The Woodsman

Michael Andrews

Michael Andrews

Cover Design: SelfPubBookCovers.com/NoveltyBookDesigns

ISBN: 9798839091894

Acknowledgements

As always, many thanks to Bex, my fabulous editor for all of your time picking up my many errors. Any that remain are purely of my design.

Thanks to S.J. Gibbs, J.M. McKenzie, Zen Grabs and Joan Gibbs for your beta reading skills.

Thanks to Martyn for coming up with an initial thought that led into this story taking fold.

Finally thanks to all my wonderful friends for your continued support through my writing adventure.

Michael Andrews

If you go down to the woods today, you're in for a big surprise.
If you go down to the woods today, you may surely die …

Michael Andrews

Chapter 1

4th July 2000

Branches scratched the face of the young boy as he ran through the thick copse of trees. He could hear the voice behind him, calling out, baiting him. Twisting and turning, the boy was running as fast as he could to escape the man chasing him but, as he turned past a tree and darted to his right, a low branch hit him square in the forehead.

Pain shot through his skull; he tried to take shallow breaths, his hand resting against the rough bark for a moment, trying to catch his breath. His hand rubbed the already prominent lump, brushing the sweat from his brow, pushing it back and upwards through the short blonde hair that was parted to the left. The cramp in his stomach twinged and the boy doubled up, spitting towards the base of the mossy trunk of the tree.

"Shit!" His stomach contracted as he dropped to

his knees. His thin body shook in a mix of fear and panic as he opened his mouth to let out a hot gush of vomit. The smell of puke assailed his nose, which caused him to heave again. The splattering of liquid against the gnarled roots of the tree sounded like an orchestra at full volume to him.

The boy tried to gulp to stem the flow of vomit in a vain effort to hide from the man chasing him. His mouth filled with bile and he swallowed, only to gag and cry out as a fresh eruption of liquid covered the forest floor.

He collapsed to the ground, the dampness of the moss cooling him as he panted loudly, tears streaming down his face. His sobs came out as loud gasps as he tried to force oxygen back into his lungs. Pushing himself back onto all fours, he felt his arms shake weakly as he tried to steady himself. He could feel the sweat puddle at the base of his spine, soaking his white school shirt. His shirt was now ruined, speckled with bloodstains from the thorny branches that he had crashed through during his attempted escape, alongside the splatters of crimson from the earlier encounter from which he was now running.

He rolled to one side, sitting back down, legs spread. He stared around blankly. He knew that the man was coming, but he could not do anything about it. His mind and body had given up. The chase was over.

The snap of twigs to his left caught his attention.

He turned his head slowly. The man was here. He had been found.

"You little fucker!" the man snarled.

The boy watched as the man walked towards him, a baseball bat in his hands. The boy had a momentary flicker of recognition but then his vision clouded. It was the Shadow Man who approached him once again.

"Please sir … don't …"

The boy felt pain like he had never experienced as the bat bounced off the side of his head. He found himself staring at the blue sky through the branches of the trees. He reached up to his forehead and brought his left hand in front of his eyes. His fingers were covered in blood. His stomach lurched and he felt warmth spread over his neck and chest as another bout of vomit covered his youthful body. He had a momentary chuckle as he thought about what his father would say about his ruined school shirt.

"What are you laughing at, boy?" the harsh voice of his assailant challenged.

"My dad is going to kill me," the boy moaned.

"You're right about that."

Heavy footsteps covered the small gap between man and boy. The boy turned his gaze, slowly, towards the oncoming man, despite the agony in his head. His vision swam and he was somewhere else, someone else.

"I'm not going to let you kill me!" The boy snarled, as a bout of strength surged through his body.

Forcing himself to his feet, the boy fumbled in the pocket of his jacket and pulled out his scout knife. Flicking it open, he thrust it upwards just as the man lurched into him. He stabbed and stabbed again, the thin blade sliding into flesh and the boy sobbed, hearing the cries of the man, before being pushed back to the ground.

"I'm gonna fucking kill you, boy!" Spittle hit the boy's face as the man shouted madly at him.

The boy felt his body lurch, as though his very soul was being wrenched from his body and, for a moment, he was looking down on the scene. The man was dressed in a padded lumberjack coat and was swinging the baseball bat wildly at the boy's prone body. He watched numbly as he saw his nose explode in a mess of blood and gristle. He heard the crack of his ribs as the man turned his attention to his chest, before the smash of his kneecaps. He watched as the bat smacked the back of his head, causing a river of red to rush down his neck. He resisted the tug of endless sleep, desperate to remain conscious, but felt his body starting to slip away.

Finally, the man dropped to his knees, the baseball bat falling from his sweaty, bloody hands.

Detached from his body, the boy saw a hunter's knife appear in the man's hand. The boy watched from above as the man placed the knife underneath the throat of his unconscious body.

The boy felt a strange, cold warmth surround him, almost as though a shadow was hugging and protecting him.

The man spat at the boy's body. "I got you, you bastard, you devil!"

Power surged through the boy's spirit. Hatred filled the empty place in his soul.

The boy opened his eyes, staring back into the man's. He coughed, a bubble of blood bursting across his lips as he let a grim smile spread across his face.

"Charlie says FUCK YOU!" the boy giggled. His hands shot upwards, grabbing the knife, and twisted it, plunging it into the heart of his attacker.

The man's body collapsed on top of him, pinning him to the ground. The boy's head throbbed, and he slipped in and out of consciousness, until blackness became his existence.

Dogs barked. Torches lit up the woods as Sammy Jacobs called to Buster, his dog, as they combed the woods looking for the missing boy. He had joined the volunteers, praying against hope that they would find the boy alive. Five boys had already been found murdered, mutilated even, and he hoped that this time, they would find this boy alive. Some of the boys had been his students. He had cried each time a new victim of the 'Woodsman' was discovered.

The police were at a loss as to who the serial killer was, but he had targeted teenage boys, chopping them to pieces in the woods. The press had jumped on it with sensationalised headlines, nicknaming him, or her, 'The Woodsman."

Buster started to pull him off to the right, away from the crowd of volunteers. The beagle's whine had an urgent pitch to it and the thirty five year old teacher allowed the dog to lead him past a heavy set of trees.

"What have you got, Buster?" Sammy said softly. "What have you found?"

Sammy stopped in his tracks as he saw the two bodies lying underneath the large oak tree.

"Oh God, please no..."

He walked towards the bodies. "Will! I think I've found something!"

Sammy slowed his steps as his brother-in-law, Will, sprinted into the opening.

The police detective watched as Sammy rolled a man's body over, uncovering the young boy underneath.

"Oh Christ, Will, he's one of mine," Sammy cried out. He reached forward, brushing the blood-soaked hair from the forehead of the youth's body. His heart sank as he looked upon the face of the twelve year old from his class and anger flared through him. "How could anyone do this to a boy?" He spat at the body of the man.

The boy's eyelids flickered open and piercing blue eyes stared back at the teacher. For a moment, Sammy was held in place, unable to drag himself away from those eyes and the pain that was locked within them. The eyelids fluttered before closing and a soft breath escaped the boy's lips.

"He's alive. Oh, thank God, he's alive!" Sammy sobbed, pulling the boy towards him.

"Sammy, don't move him. He looks in a bad way. You could make any injuries worse," DS Will Michaels said as he touched his brother in law's shoulder.

Sammy laid the boy back down softly before rocking back, sitting on his ankles as he continued to stare into the now closed eyes of the young boy.

"You know the boy?" Will asked.

"Yeah… this is one of my students, nice lad, quiet lad. His name is Zachary Downes."

Will Michaels stared at the body of the dead man, his heart pounding in his chest.

"This is Harvey Downes," Will hissed. He saw the

blood on the man's hands and the stab wounds in his chest. "This is Zachary's father."

Other police officers poured into the small clearing. A female policewoman knelt beside the boy, checking his vitals.

"Detective, we need an ambulance. The boy is unresponsive," she said.

Will heard his radio buzz. "What?" he snapped into it. "It's not a good time."

"Boss. You need to get to the Downes' house!" The voice of Sergeant Lowry came across the radio.

"No need," Will sighed. "We've found the boy and his father in the woods."

"Boss. There's another son, Kenny. He's been, well, I don't know how to describe it."

Will could hear retching from the radio.

"The boy has been chopped up, boss. Just like the others."

Will Michaels stared at the two bodies, wondering what would cause a father to murder his son and try to kill his other, let alone those other poor boys.

Chapter 2

4th May 2021

"It's with great pleasure that I would like to introduce Detective Constable Zack Jacobs to the team." Detective Inspector Will Michaels said as he shook his adopted nephew's hand. The thirty three year old smiled nervously at the assembled group of detectives.

"Thank you, sir," Zack caught himself from addressing his new boss as uncle. *That wouldn't have been a good start,* he smiled to himself.

"Zack, you've finally made it out of grunt work," DS Paula Smith smiled. "You're my desk buddy." She pointed to the empty chair on the pod next to hers. "Make yourself at home and I'll show you where the kettle is."

"I thought I'd left tea-making behind," Zack half-joked.

"Oh no! Newbie still makes the drinks," a voice from behind startled him. Turning, Zack smiled and took the hand of a blonde-haired man.

"Police Constable Hemmings, it's good to see you again."

"Lay off it, Zack," Bobby Hemmings cringed. "I only failed the exam by three points."

"Still, Police Constable, I'll have two sugars in my coffee." The pair slapped each other on the arms and, after the drinks had been made, Zack settled down at his desk. He opened his backpack and put out the family photos that he carried with him.

The first, a black framed picture of his adopted father, Sammy Jacobs, smiling as the pair held a large koi carp that Zack had caught on their first holiday as father and son. Zack's hair was cut short, the scar of the brain surgery still visible. He ran his hand through his now curly blonde hair.

The second was a picture of a younger Zack, taken on his twelfth birthday. His older brother Kenny had an infectious smile and his arm around his younger brother. It was the last photo that had been taken of the two brothers before Kenny's murder.

DI Michaels walked up to the desk. He picked up the photo of Zack and Sammy. "This was the first fishing holiday, wasn't it," he said. "I remember Sam asking to borrow my boat. How is he? Any improvement?"

"No Uncle Will, erm … sorry. No boss." Zack cursed himself.

"Look Zack, it will take some time to get used to calling me boss, so we'll expect the occasional slip up," Will smiled. "Just try not to do it in front of the others or you'll be given hell for weeks. Have you been to see Sammy recently?"

"It's hard," Zack said. "He doesn't even recognise me anymore."

"Dementia is a hard condition to deal with but remember, you know him. It has been proven to help bring them back to us. I'm going to pop in on the way home tonight."

"I'll go tomorrow." Zack knew that he would not.

Sighing to himself, Will walked to the front of the office and called everyone to attention. Turning to the wall mounted monitor, he flicked the power button on the remote and a grisly scene greeted the detectives.

"Okay people, listen up. We have a nasty one here."

"Aren't they always," Paula sniffed.

"Mary Hopkins, 37, battered to death. Prime suspect is her husband Richard Hopkins, 36. Nasty piece of work. Four prior allegations of domestic assault; three dismissed through lack of evidence; one conviction with community service as the punishment. His first wife was also murdered, and he was investigated by Bristol CID, but they were unable to get enough evidence to convict him. It was a hung jury, and the judge dismissed the case. CPS have never been able to proceed from there."

"Fucking judges!"

"DS Smith, please keep your opinions to yourself." Will reprimanded her. "Even if they are valid."

"This is why we need that register, but the damn Tories voted it down again."

"What register?" Zack asked his new colleague.

"We've been pushing for a domestic violence register, similar to the sex offender one, but with looser access. Women could check if their new partners have history."

"Well, he's now in custody, having handed himself in, but we need to make sure he doesn't get away with it this time." DI Michaels sat down heavily. "I want us to cross all the T's and dot all the I's on this. No mistakes."

Zack was flicking through the folder. "Where's the boy?"

"What boy?" Will asked.

"It says here that they have a fourteen year old son, Daniel."

"He's with his uncle," Bobby stated. "Jamie Whitehall. The son is the one who found his mother when he got home from school, according to the locals. The neighbours called us when they heard him scream."

"Okay, lets split up. Paula, you're with me," Will said. "We'll go to the scene and see what forensics have found. Zack, you take Bobby and go and interview the son."

With a round of 'okay boss' echoing in the office, the team headed for their cars and respective appointments. As Zack and Bobby reached the car, Bobby held out the keys.

"You drive, Bobby," Zack muttered. "I want to have a read of the file again before we get there."

"Sure thing."

The car weaved slowly through the early morning traffic, as the people of Bristol made their daily trek to work. Zack had his head down, studying the file. The boy's smiling face in the school photograph tugged at a memory in Zack, but he could not place it.

"It's getting busier again, now that the restrictions are easing," Bobby interrupted his thoughts.

"Huh?"

"I was just saying … are you okay? You look like you've seen a ghost."

"I'm fine," Zack answered, although he felt a shiver running down his spine. Pulling down the sun visor, he looked in the small mirror. He did not recognise his eyes for a moment, almost as though the bright blue pigment of his iris had darkened, but he shook it off. "I skipped breakfast because I slept through my alarm," he added. "I'll grab a snack on the way back from the Whitehall house."

"If you're sure … HEY! Watch it kid!" Bobby yelled out of his window as he swerved to avoid a young lad on a bike, who had ridden into the road from between two parked cars.

Zack sniggered to himself as the boy, who's hoodie had fallen off to reveal a shock of red hair, mouthed an obvious string of swear words and stuck his middle finger up at the pair. Bobby started to slow the car down.

"Let it go, Bobby. We need to get Daniel's statement, remember."

"Fine. I just hate the little shits who flip us the bird. No respect for us anymore."

"We're in plain clothes and in an unmarked car," Zack reminded him. "We're just a couple of guys to him."

"Still … nothing that a good slap wouldn't sort."

Zack felt the shiver run down his back again. He raised his hand to his eyes as his vision blurred. He rubbed his hand across his forehead as a pain shot through his temples.

"What do you mean by that, Zack?" Bobby's voice

was tempered, as though through gritted teeth.

"Mean by what?"

"You just snapped my head off, saying that you'd batter me if I laid a hand on the boy."

"I didn't say anything of the sort. I said that we're plain clothes, and then I felt a bit funny again."

Bobby slowed the car and pulled to the side of the road. "Mate, you've gone pale again. There's a McDonald's up ahead. I think we should swing through and get you a McMuffin or something."

"Yeah … I think you're right."

They sat in silence as they waited in the small queue at the drive through. Zack's eyes were fixed on the car in front, trying to avoid any conversation. Bobby glanced across at his friend. "Two double sausage and egg McMuffins please," he said as the server's voice crackled through the mic.

"I'll get these," Zack said, pulling out a ten-pound note from his wallet. "Have it as an apology for whatever I said back there."

Bobby handed the money to the server, telling her to keep the change, and pulled into a lay-by. The smell of the food caused his stomach to rumble, and the pair giggled like schoolboys, breaking the tension for a moment.

"Sorry about that." Zack said, rubbing his stomach. He looked at Bobby, whose expression had turned serious once again.

"You can't remember what you said?" Bobby asked, concern in his voice.

"I honestly think that I didn't say anything, but if you're saying that I did, then it may have been a blank moment."

"A blank moment? Like you used to get when we were kids?"

"I've not had one since I came out of the coma after, you know, what my father did," Zack frowned. "I thought that maybe the head injury had actually sorted it out."

"Well, let's get this interview over with and we'll go for a pint after work."

"It's okay Bobby …"

"Look Zack. You're my best mate and have been since we were at St James' school. We were, what? Nine?"

"I was ten. You were a couple of months short of your birthday. We got into that fight with the older kids, a couple of Kenny's friends, if I remember."

"Oh, Christ yes! Wait … give me that file for a sec."

Bobby flicked through the pages; his brow furrowed.

"What are you looking for."

"You've reminded me of him. Look!"

Zack studied at the mugshot of the accused. "What am I looking at, other than the bastard who battered his wife."

"Look at the scar on his left cheek."

"So, he has a scar. He probably got it in a fight, if his record is anything to go by."

"He did get it in a fight. You gave it him."

"What?"

"Your eleventh birthday, remember? Tricky Dicky Hopkins, everyone at school used to call him that."

Zack stared hard at the photo. He tried to imagine the stern looking criminal as a young boy but failed. He shrugged and put the photo back into the file.

"Must be one of the things that I've forgotten," Zack said. He flinched as white-hot pain shot through his temple.

"Maybe you should stay in the car when we get to the Whitehall house."

"I'll be fine. I used to get these migraines when I was a kid. We'll stop off at a pharmacy on the way back to the station and I'll grab some co-codamol."

"Whatever you say, boss."

Bobby turned into a quiet cul-de-sac and slowed the car down to a crawl. Zack pointed towards a house with a blue Ford Fiesta parked on the drive.

"It's that one," he said, the reopened file on his lap. "Remember, kid gloves with the boy."

Bobby grunted as they pulled up. They walked up the driveway and knocked on the door. Zack squinted as the morning sun started to make his headache worse. The door opened and a middle-aged man, with dark rings under his eyes, greeted them.

"Mr Whitehall? I'm PC Hemmings, this is DC Jacobs," Bobby flashed his police ID and Zack pulled his out of his back pocket.

"We've been expecting you," Jamie Whitehall sighed. "Please, come in. Bren... can you put the kettle on, the police are here," he said, turning towards a slim brunette. She nodded.

"Sugar? Milk?"

"Just milk for me, love," Bobby said.

"Could I just grab some water please?" Zack said. "I don't suppose I could trouble you for a couple of paracetamols?"

"Sure thing, Detective," Brenda smiled at him.

Jamie led them through a door into the lounge, gesturing for them to sit. "Do you want to talk to Dan straight away, or can we help out first?"

"Well, we are here to get his statement," Bobby started before he saw Zack raise his hand slightly.

"How is he?" Zack asked. "I'm sure that this must be hard for him."

"He's doing surprisingly well," Brenda said, carrying in a tray of drinks and placing it on the low, wooden coffee table. She winced slightly as she took her seat. "He was always a lot closer to Richard than Mary…"

"But that still doesn't mean he isn't upset by what that swine has done to my sister." Jamie hissed.

Zack sat back into the chair, picking up the two small, round pills and popped them into his mouth, taking a swig of the ice-cold water to swallow them down. "Maybe you could tell us a little about the dynamics before we talk to Danny."

"Dan." Jamie said. "He hates being called Danny."

"Good lord, he does," Brenda said, rubbing her side. "But Dan is a lovely lad. I can't believe that he had to see what he did."

"So, do you know any reason why Richard would want to harm Mary?" Zack asked.

"What, other than him being a bastard?" Jamie hissed.

"Don't you talk about my dad like that!"

They all turned to see a dark-haired teenager standing in the doorway. His face was in a scowl and Zack stiffened immediately.

21

"Dan, we were just…" Jamie started.

"I know what you were 'just doing', Uncle Jamie," the boy hissed. "You never liked Dad, and now you are trying to blame him for what happened to her."

"Dan, is it?" Zack started. "No-one is trying to blame your dad."

"Sure, that's why you're here, having arrested his ass?"

"Dan, I bet it's just like Line of Duty or something," a young voice said from behind the tall teenager. A smaller, mousey haired boy crept past him and took a seat next to Jamie.

"Don't be so stupid!" Dan's voice dripped with contempt. "I can't believe you're so retarded."

"Daniel! We've asked you not to call him that!" Brenda snapped, standing up. The teenager shot her a look, and she sat back down, putting her arm around her son as she pulled him into her lap.

"This is our son, Philip," she said to Zack and Bobby. "He likes watching all of the police dramas."

"They're all so fucking stupid," Dan laughed. "Nothing works out like they show on telly."

"Okay, I think we all need to step back for a moment and cool down," Bobby said softly. "Dan, we need to ask you about what happened when you got home from school yesterday."

"What do you need to know? The stupid bitch

had fallen over drunk again and this time, she hit her head."

Zack noticed the change in posture of the others as the boy spouted his contempt for his stepmother.

"Dan, you know that she had her drinking under control," Jamie said softly.

"Like fuck!" the boy snapped backed. "She couldn't handle the fact that I liked going out with Dad, and that my mates would come round."

"You do know that you shouldn't have had people round your house during the lockdown?" Zack said.

"Yeah right," the boy chuckled. "Everyone was doing it, and you pigs couldn't do fuck all about it."

Bobby threw Zack a look that showed his disgust. Zack shook his head at his friend and turned back to the fourteen year old.

"Obviously, you must be upset about your mother, so we will let that go for now," he started. "But we do need to get your account of the situation when you got home from school yesterday. We have a witness statement saying that you got home around 4pm. Is that correct?"

"Dan, we bunked off the last couple of lessons to come back here to play on Call of Duty," Philip piped up. "You and the others left before Dad got home at three."

"Shut up, you retard." Dan looked over at the adults. "Okay, we skipped school but that's 'cos this idiot wanted to play his stupid game. Doesn't mean anything."

"Of course, it doesn't," Jamie said, patting Dan's knee. The boy flinched away from the touch.

"So, can you tell us what happened when you got home?" Zack asked, pulling his notebook from his jacket pocket.

"It's simple," the boy started. "I left here at three…" he shot a look at his cousin. "I phoned my girl on the way home and met her, and we, you know, snogged for a bit and a little more." Dan giggled and groped his crotch. "I wanted to go back to hers, but she wasn't alone, so I went back home and found the bitch dead on the floor."

"And where was your father?" Bobby asked.

"Fuck knows…" Dan shrugged. "He must have run somewhere as you bastards would think he had done it."

"Why would that be?" Zack asked.

"'Cos of the trouble he's had before. But I will tell you now, Dad had nothing to do with that bitch's death."

"Stop calling her that," Jamie stood up and strode towards his nephew. His face was red with anger. Bobby and Zack jumped up and got in between them.

24

"Fuck you, Uncle Jamie," Dan shouted. "You know she was a no-good drunk!"

"And why do you think that was, you little piece of shit."

"Fuck you!"

"DAD!" Philip yelled and jumped up.

Zack did not see the first of the punches thrown, but he heard the thud as Philip hit the floor, holding his face. Zack moved forwards and got in the middle of them, grabbing Dan and turning him so that his body was in between the boy and his uncle.

"Okay, you're both under arrest," Bobby said, wrestling Jamie to the ground, flipping him onto his back and handcuffing him.

"Ha! Serves you right, you bastard," Dan sneered before Zack approached him. "What?"

"You too, son," he said apologetically. "Let's get down the station and we can sort all of this out."

"You're fucking kidding me?"

"I'm afraid not. You've assaulted your uncle and cousin in front of us, so we need to process it. Look, I'm sure we can get it all sorted out, because of the trauma of your mother's death, so let's take it easy and not make me handcuff you, okay?"

"Whatever."

Bobby had already radioed in for a couple of cars

to come in and help split the pair up for the journey back to the station.

As the uniformed officers arrived, and Bobby was supervising walking the pair from the house to put Dan and Jamie in separate cars, Zack turned to Brenda.

"I'm sorry this escalated like this. All we wanted was to find out what Dan walked in on, so that we can proceed with our investigation against Richard."

"It wasn't Uncle Richard," Philip mumbled.

"Pardon?"

"Dan's nasty," the young boy stammered. "I think that he killed Auntie Mary."

"Philip, don't say such things," Brenda gasped.

"Mum, you know he hit her, and he ..." Tears started to dribble down Philip's cheeks. He lifted his shirt and turned his back to Zack and Brenda.

"He told me to say that he was here till four, like the neighbours said. He said he'd hurt me worse if I didn't, but I know ... I know it was him."

Brenda cried out and rushed to hug her young son.

The sight of purple bruises and cigarette burns on the pale skin of the boy's back made Zack feel sick.

Chapter 3

June 2000

"Leave me alone!" Zachary cried as he was held down by the three older boys. His blonde hair was matted with mud and his sun-kissed cheeks were streaked with salty rivers of tears.

"Oh look, the little baby is crying," Ian Hollis laughed as he strode over and sat on the younger boy, straddling his waist. He looked up at his two friends who were holding the younger boy's arms and legs, so that he could not move. He leaned in close to the boy's face. "You're such a little pussy, I bet you like me sitting on you, don't you! I bet you want me to kiss you."

The young boy flinched as he felt the tongue of the older bully lick his cheeks, before pulling away slightly. He cringed as the older boy hocked a cough in his mouth and spat out a wad of phlegm. It dribbled down the boy's cheeks. Suddenly, he gasped and started to struggle under the weight of the older boy as he felt a hand start to grope his groin.

"He likes this shit!" Jason Billings chuckled, stroking his hand up and down the boy's shorts. "Let's strip him."

Sniggers rang out and Zachary twisted. Seeing Peter Kenton pushing Jason in a jokey manner, he cried out.

"NO! Please, leave me alone."

"Shut up, you little pussy!" Ian shouted as he slapped the young boy's face. The echo of the slap rang out across the small copse of trees, and he repeated it. Slap after slap rang out, and the small boy's cheeks turned red under the assault.

Zachary knew that he was helpless, but when he felt the hands on the button and the zip of his grey school shorts, he threw his body upwards with all his might. The boy on top of him was thrown to one side, cursing when his hip hit the upturned tree trunk.

The younger boy scrambled to his feet, holding his shorts up, but his escape was a dream as his body was slammed from behind, and he was thrown back onto the ground. Fists pummelled into his back, and he cried out in agony, and he felt a rib crack under the assault.

Zachary managed to turn himself over and raised

his arms up to protect his face as the three boys were joined by three more.

"Kenny, please. Don't." The boy's voice was barely a whisper.

"You killed my mother, you fucker!" A face full of hatred confronted him, and the smaller boy felt spittle hit his face. He tried to raise his arms to wipe it off, but his wrists were being held down once again. Kenny punched his younger brother's face over and over until the body underneath him stopped struggling.

Kenny looked down at the helpless boy and, for a moment, he could see his mother's face; one that he had only known in photographs, staring back at him. A feeling of love rushed through him, and he leaned down, wrapping his arms around the prone body. "I'm sorry Mum," he whispered. He shook his head and saw the bloodied face of his younger brother.

"Shit," Kenny said, kneeling up before getting off his brother's unconscious body. "My dad is gonna kill me if he finds out I've beaten him like this."

"He's a little shit," Ian sniggered. "I know he's a fucking queer."

"Don't you say that!" Kenny hissed; fists clenched turning to his friend. "My brother isn't a fag."

"He must be," Jason laughed. He reached down and pulled the young boy's shorts and underwear down. "Look, he's got a boner from me feeling him up."

"You're the fucking queer," Kenny grabbed his friend's shirt, pulling him close so that their faces were inches apart. "And if I ever see you touching him up again, I'll fucking kill you."

"Jeezus, okay!" Jason stepped back. "I was just joking and hazing him."

"Yeah right," George Adams said, brushing his dark hair away from his eyes. "You've been messing around with your brother."

"Have not!"

"Have so!"

"What the fuck? Your brother is like, what, ten?" Kenny spat at his friend. "You ever touch Zack like that again, and I swear to God, I will cut off your dick and shove it down your throat!"

"I thought that you hated him?" Jason started to back away from the group, sensing that they had turned on him.

"We don't like perverts," Dicky Hopkins stepped in. "After Mr. Gregory raped that boy last year, you should know that."

"I haven't," Jason stammered. "I wouldn't."

"Just fuck off now, or I'll chop every part of your body into pieces, and they will need miles of duct tape to put you back together again," Kenny said, a soft tone to his voice making the threat sound all the more menacing.

The boys watched as their friend turned and ran from the woods.

"So, do you think he's a fag?" Jack Cowell asked slowly.

"Jason is a fucking pervert," George said. "I was staying at his house on his birthday, and he got his brother naked and was playing with him."

"No, I meant him," Jack said, kicking the unconscious boy. "I hate fags."

"I'm no fag," a croaky voice startled the boys. "I'll fucking kill anyone who says I am."

Kenny looked down into the blue eyes of his younger brother. His face had a scowl that Kenny had not seen before. Leaning down, he picked up his skinny brother, his weight nothing to the athletic youth.

"I need to get him home," Kenny said. "I don't want my dad to bawl on me."

"He's bleeding a lot," Dicky said, concern in his voice. "Maybe we need to stop some of it, before we take him back to yours."

Kenny looked at his friend. "Okay Tricky, you know about medical shit. You do that St Johns Ambulance thing." He laid his younger brother back down on the mossy ground and Dicky Hopkins pulled out his handkerchief. Licking the white cotton material, the boy dabbed at the cuts on the younger boy's face. He wiped the blood away from the brow and mouth of the boy.

Zachary stirred on the ground and opened his eyes. He felt the soft touch of Dicky as the older boy cleaned up his face. His eyes met those of the older boy and the younger boy saw affection, or at least, sorrow.

"I hurt," Zachary whispered.

"Where?" Dicky asked.

"My chest."

Dicky ran his hands softly over the younger boy's chest, moving them inside his shirt.

"Eh? Tricky… are you a fucking pervert as well?" George yelled, kicking his friend.

"No! I think we've broken his ribs."

"So what?" Kenny said. "Let's just get him back to my house and he can fucking piss his bed, like he normally does."

"Mate, I think he's hurt bad," Dicky said.

"Fuck me, you fucking fancy him?" George accused.

"Fuck you! I think we need to take him to a hospital."

"He'll be fine," Kenny said gruffly. "Let's just get him home."

As the boys entered the house, Dicky carried Zachary through the kitchen and into his bedroom. He laid him onto his bed and took off the boy's school shoes and paused for a moment. He glanced around and seeing that the other boys had stayed in the kitchen, he leaned over the battered boy.

"I'm so sorry, Zack," he whispered into his ear. "I'll try to protect you." The boy turned towards him, his watery eyes open.

"I trust you," The younger boy said. "But you guys hurt me."

"It won't happen again, if I can help it."

"What the fuck has been going on?" The voice of Harvey Downes broke the moment. Dicky turned and saw his friend's father standing in the doorway.

"Zack fell over in the woods on the way home," he lied. "I think he's hurt his ribs."

"Well, the little sod can just suck it up like real men do," Harvey said, popping the top of the bottle of beer that was in his right hand. Taking a long swig, he let out a burp and turned away.

"Thank you for helping me," Zachary whispered as Dicky left the room. He felt a cold sensation run through his body. "I'll remember what you did."

Dicky turned, thinking that he had heard another boy in the room but only saw Zachary as he closed his eyes and fell into an uncomfortable sleep.

Chapter 4

May 2021

"Mother of God!" DI Michaels moaned. "I thought that we had the suspect in custody, but now you've brought in two more."

"I know boss," Zack sighed. "We had to arrest them both for assault on each other, but we can bail them out straight away. Especially the boy."

"I'm not so sure gaffer," Bobby started. "I think the boy is a wrong 'un."

"What do you mean?" Will Michaels asked.

"The way he was calling his mum …"

"Some boys fall out with them," Zack said.

"Then there is the fact that I think he had assaulted his aunt …"

"This is only coming up now?" Zack asked.

"His cousin is scared shitless of him, and the boy threatened him. You saw the bruises on Philip's body."

"Look, we have the prime suspect in custody," Zack said. "We just need to get the statement from Daniel that he saw his father kill her, and it's a closed case."

"Whilst I'm inclined to agree with DC Jacobs, I'm not so sure," Will started before sitting down heavily in his chair. He picked up the file which was getting heavier by the minute. He scratched his head, his fingernails running through the short, buzz cut hair. "I've read Bobby's report and I'm concerned about the boy, Danny?"

"Dan, or Daniel," Zack interjected.

"Zack, I want you to run a full check on him, school records, any closed police records, the whole works. Use my authority if you have to, but I want to have a full report on him. Bobby, if you have a moment."

Zack grunted, nodded, and left the office. Bobby sat down in the offered seat.

"I know that you and Zack go way back, even before the police, but I need to ask you what happened today."

Bobby frowned and rubbed his temples. "Boss, I don't know, honestly."

"What you say here is off the record," Will said. "You know my relationship with Zack, so you know I'm looking out for him. One of the uniforms mentioned that he threatened Jamie Whitehall if he hurt the boy."

"What?" Bobby asked. "I didn't hear that."

"I believe you were loading the kid into the other car at the time."

Bobby sat back, rocking the chair slightly. He was stuck in the moment of truth, the moment of betraying a friend, or being dishonest to his boss.

"On the way there, a kid rode out in front of us, and we nearly knocked him off his bike. He flipped us the bird and I shouted at him. Zack, well, he threatened me, but has no recollection of it."

"You haven't put that in your report."

"Of course, I haven't. I'm not gonna snitch on my mate and get him into trouble," Bobby hissed. "He can't remember it, and well, he used to get memory loss as a kid when all that shit was going on, when his father was killing them boys."

Will nodded. "He's not had an episode since Sammy adopted him. Let's keep this between us for now, but do me a favour, keep your eye on him."

"Sure thing, boss."

The interview room was a stark, soulless room. The walls were painted grey, and the only furniture was a plain wooden table, surrounded by four chairs that were fully occupied.

"Now just relax, Dan," Zack said. "This is going to be quick and easy."

"Whatever."

Zack glanced at Paula, hearing that the usual arrogant sneer in the boy's voice had taken a small backstep as Dan's eyes darted around the bleak room.

"Is this the first time you've been in an interview room?"

"I think we should wait until the tape starts before you start asking him questions." Zack sighed as the words from the duty lawyer stopped him in his tracks.

"Come on, Harry," Paula sighed, glancing at the lawyer. "We're just getting him comfortable before we start."

"Don't say anything until the recording starts and then, let me guide you." The grey-haired man sat next to Dan placed his hand on the boy's arm. Dan looked up at him and the arrogant sneer came back across his face.

Paula reached over and pressed the record button on the tape machine. The room was silent as three bleeps were followed by a longer one.

"This is a witness interview into the investigation of the murder of Mary Hopkins. Present are: DS

Paula Smith, DC Zachary Jacobs, Harry Gillespie, duty solicitor and acting in loco parentis, and a child under the age of sixteen, who will be referred to as Child A."

"I'm not a child," Dan snapped.

"Sorry son," Zack said. "It is a term that we have to use to protect your anonymity in case we have enough evidence to proceed to trial."

"I'm not gonna snitch on my dad, so you can fuck off. He would have still been at work anyway, he's always at work."

"Hush," Harry said, touching Dan's arm.

"Get your hands off me, perv."

"Let's calm down," Zack said. He held out a bottle of water to the boy. "Take a swig and a breath."

"Got anything stronger?" Dan chuckled before taking the bottle. He tried to twist the top but flinched. Zack took the bottle back, broke the plastic seal and handed it back.

"How did you hurt your hand?" Paula asked.

"Got in a fight at school."

"With whom?"

"What's that matter?"

"Do you get into lots of fights?"

"Excuse me, but what does that have to do with why we are here?" Harry asked.

"We're just after a sense of character."

"No, you're not. You're fishing for anything that could implicate my client in the murder. He is here purely as a witness, and if you stray from that line of questioning, this interview is over."

"Yeah... what he said." Dan leaned back in his chair, a smile creeping onto his face. "Sorry for calling you a perv... you're okay."

Zack leaned forward. "Okay, let's stick to the witness information then. Can you tell us what happened on the afternoon of May 3rd?"

"What's to tell that I didn't say already to the coppers. I got home from school and saw Mary on the floor dead."

"Now, we know that's not true," Paula said. "You told DC Jacobs that you bunked off school, something we have confirmed with the school."

"Oh, for fuck's sake. Yeah, I went to my cousin's to play Call of Duty and then went home and found her."

"Who else bunked off with you?"

"You don't need to answer that," Harry interrupted.

"It's not a crime to bunk off," Paula said. "We just want to corroborate the timeline of the child's movement."

"You have already received that from his cousin."

"Yeah, that little retard dobbed me in," Dan snapped.

"How do you feel about that?" Paula asked.

"You know what they say? Snitches get stitches," Dan laughed.

"It wouldn't be the first time you've hit your cousin, would it?"

"Don't answer!" Harry raised his voice. "This is straying from the agreed questioning."

"Sorry," Paula lowered her eyes to her notes. "Okay, you left your cousin's house at what time?"

"Three. I went to meet a girl."

"Her name?"

"No comment," Dan smirked. "Her husband doesn't know about us."

Zack and Paula looked at each other, their eyes asking the same questions.

"Don't answer anything else about that," Harry said, leaning into the boy. "I think that I need to have a consultation with my client before we continue."

Paula nodded at Zack who leaned over to stop the recording. "One last question before we stop the tape. In all the interviews, you have never called Mary Hopkins your mother."

"'Cos she's not!" Dan spat. "She moved in six

months after my Mum died, like she was just waiting for her to die. I'm glad she's dead. She was a bitch."

"This interview is over for now." Harry stood up.

Zack stopped the recording, and the pair left the room.

"Well, he's a little shit, isn't he," Paula said as they walked down the corridor towards the small kitchen.

"He's an angry fourteen year old who has just seen his mother killed," Zack countered.

"Not his mother, as he was very keen to point out."

"It can be a normal reaction to a step-parent, or an adopted one."

"Sorry, Zack. I keep forgetting." Paula touched his arm. "But I've worked with enough angry teenagers to know when they are in mourning or when they do actually hate someone."

"Hate is a strong word."

"Okay, fine. How about dislike strongly." She offered a half smile.

They walked into the open plan office and DI Michaels motioned for them to come to his office. Closing the door behind them, they took the offered seats.

"How's it going with the kid?"

"He's a snotty little bastard, but Zack seems to like him," Paula smirked. "Must be the new kid on the block empathy."

"Ha. Funny." Zack scowled. "There's a lot more going on with him than we first thought. I'd agree with Paula that he isn't a nice, clean-cut kid, but he's just thrown in that he is vulnerable, as he claims to be in a sexual relationship with a married woman."

"What?" DI Michaels rubbed his hand over his face. "Any hints as to whom?"

"Wouldn't say, and his duty lawyer is …"

"Let me guess … Harry Gillespie. Why does he always want to be a thorn in our side?"

"Who is he? Dan pegged him as a perv at first, now he's his best mate," Zack asked.

"He jumps onto cases and throws spanners into our investigations, even on the simplest ones," DI Michaels said.

"Whole toolboxes sometimes," Paula agreed. "Why he's come onto this one, God only knows."

"Even so, getting back to the boy," DI Michaels started. "Do you think he's being abused?"

"I'm not sure. My gut says no, and that maybe he's, at least, a willing participant. However, it could be that he is giving it 'the big I am', putting on the bravado to hide the abuse," Zack said reluctantly. "Sometimes I know that I've got blinkers on when it comes to protecting kids, but I'd have to say that I am beginning to agree that he isn't a saint."

"Could it be related in any way to the Mary Hopkins' murder?" DI Michaels asked.

"How?"

"Maybe she found out and confronted him?"

"Or maybe she is the married woman?" Paula queried.

"His own mother?" DI Michaels groaned.

"Step-mother," she replied.

"Maybe Richard came home, found them together and lost the plot." DI Michaels offered.

"I don't know," Zack frowned. He scratched his head. The itch that had been bothering him most of the day was getting worse. "I'd like to see what Richard says first."

"Thank you both. Zack, can you stay for a moment," DI Michaels said.

Paula nodded and left the office. Zack looked over at the DI.

"I don't want you to be involved in anything where Richard Hopkins is involved."

"Why?"

"There are reasons, but mostly connected to your past. You know that I was involved in the Woodsman case. Richard was one of your brother's friends and, as it was them who your, erm, who Harvey killed, I think there is a chance that, if he recognises you, he is going to try to play on that."

"How could he?"

"Bullies thrive on getting under people's skin, winding them up, make them react like they wouldn't normally. If he gets you to speak out of turn, or worse, hit him, the whole case collapses under PCC investigations."

Zack frowned. "Okay, I get it. I've only just figured out who he was anyway, and trust me, I have no intention of wanting to be in the same room as him."

"Thanks Zack. Why don't you and Paula go back and probe the kid for more information about this married woman, and I'll let you know about what we get from Hopkins."

Chapter 5

June 2000

Sirens echoed around the neighbourhood as Zachary peered out of his bedroom window. The flashing blue lights had woken him up as they lit up the night sky. He jumped out of his bed, pulling up his pyjama bottoms that threatened to fall from his slim waist. Tugging them up, Zachary opened his curtains and watched the scene on the street below.

"This looks like something out of a movie," he said in awe before turning at the sound of his bedroom door opening.

"What's going on, retard," Kenny hissed at him, barging him to one side.

"Somethings happening at Jason's house."

"What do you mean?" The older boy looked at his brother.

"Look, there's loads of police there. Maybe

they've figured out he was messing around with his brother, Nate."

"You shut up about that," Kenny snarled, punching Zachary in the side. "Jason's not a pervert."

"He is so," Zachary said softly, rubbing his side. "He, um, well, he, you know."

Kenny stared at him, his face hardening. "Where were you earlier anyway? You weren't at home when I got back from school. Were you with him?"

"No. I was just…" Zachary paused, his face scrunching up in thought. "I was just walking home. I guess I was just thinking about stuff, 'cos I left school and the next thing I knew, I was getting out of the shower."

"I need to know if you lied about him touching you?" Kenny grabbed his younger brother. The older boy could see the tears trickling down his brother's cheeks. Zachary looked up at his older brother, hoping to see compassion in his siblings' eyes but knowing that he would not. He wiped away the tears, wincing as he touched the still healing bruises from the beating in the woods that his brother had given him three days before.

"He never did that. I wouldn't let him." Zachary's voice had a dangerous edge to it.

Kenny was taken aback for a moment by the change in his brother's voice. They both jumped as the smack of the bedroom door broke the silence between them.

"Has who touched who?" Their Dad slurred as he staggered into his youngest son's bedroom. "Is someone messing around with you, boy?"

He grabbed Zachary by his cotton pyjama top and lifted him from his feet. Zachary blanched as he could smell the whisky on his dad's breath.

"You told me you weren't one of them faggot boys, so who is making you do stuff?"

"Dad, I'm not, and no-one has," Zachary cried. "Please, I've not done anything wrong."

Harvey Downes looked his youngest in the eyes and seeing fear, not guilt, he smiled and threw the boy onto his bed. "Well, if it was the fucking Billings boy, you don't need to worry about him touching you anymore. He's dead by all accounts. Chopped up and left in the woods."

"Good," Kenny smiled. "Hope he suffered, fucking perv."

"That's not right," Zachary sniffled. "He was still a person."

Harvey snorted. "You stay here, and I'll go check what's going on," he said. He staggered towards the door before tripping and falling over the small cabinet that housed Zachary's Star Wars figure collection. A string of curses made even Kenny blanch, and the boy decided he needed to distract his father.

"Dad, maybe I should go and ask?" Kenny suggested.

"Good idea, son," His father smiled. As his eldest son left, he turned to his youngest, who was still crying on his bed. "Maybe one day you'll grow some balls and act like a man, like your brother, rather than the fucking girl you are."

Zachary wiped his eyes. He watched as his father pushed himself to his feet. Zachary felt faint, as though he was somewhere else for a moment. His legs felt weak and, as he tried to stand, he had to sit down quickly before he fell over.

"What the fuck did you just say to me, boy?" Harvey yelled, striding over to his youngest son. Two loud slaps showed his displeasure, and he heard his boy cry out. He thought, *that's better. Boys should respect their father. I can't believe he just called me those names. He needs to learn respect!*

"I didn't say anything, Daddy," the young boy cried back.

"Well, it's time you learned your place."

Harvey unbuckled his belt and folded it in two, swatting it on his hand.

Kenny walked back slowly from his friend's house, thoughts tumbling through his mind. Jason had been his friend since they were nine years old, but the last couple of years, he had turned weird. With what he had found out, Kenny had tried to distance himself from Jason, but the boy would not let go. As much as he hated his brother for killing his Mum, he loved him enough that he would not let a pervert molest him.

The numerous policemen had stopped him from going up to the house, but he was clever enough to remember the secret routes they had made years before.

Kenny had easily climbed up Old Man Claridge's tree and jumped over the fence into the Billings' back garden. It was simple enough to scoot over to the lounge window. Easing the left-hand window open, Kenny looked in and listened to the conversation that was taking place inside.

"I'm very sorry, Mr Billings," a tall, plain clothed policeman started. "We have found a body in the woods, and well, we have identified it as Jason."

"Are you sure, Will?" Eric Billings asked. There was a tremble in his voice that Kenny had never heard before. Janet Billings was crying, her arms wrapped around her younger son, Nate.

"He's dead?" the boy asked. His face was stoic, his voice steady and emotionless.

"I'm afraid so," Will Michaels nodded.

"Good." A tear trickled down the boy's cheek.

"Nate! Both Janet and Eric looked at him, aghast.

"He'd been doing stuff to me, so I don't care," the boy shouted. "Whoever did this has done me a massive favour. I want to find him to say thank you."

"Now, I'm sure that emotions are running high," Will started.

"No. Nate, you take that back. Your brother was a good boy, and he didn't deserve to be killed." Janet shook her youngest.

"He was doing sex stuff to me," Nate said quietly, his voice so soft that all the adults in the room stopped. His voice was steady, his teeth clenched. "He deserved to die."

"Nate, you can't say things like that" Eric said. "Jason was a good boy," he stated, turning to the policemen in the room.

Kenny saw his friend's brother stiffen but Nate remained silent.

"How did he die?" Nate asked finally.

"I'm not sure if it's appropriate," Will started.

"You want to know what happened to your brother?" Janet screamed, pushing her son away from her. "He was chopped up into pieces and left in the woods."

Nate stepped back for a moment. "All of him was

chopped up?"

"What do you mean?" Will asked softly, sensing that Nate was telling the truth about the abuse from his older brother.

"Did someone cut off his dick?"

"NATE!"

Will grabbed Janet's arm as soon as she had left her handprint on the young boy's face. Nate cried out in shock, holding his own hand to his face to try to calm the stinging pain in his cheek.

"I hope whoever did it, did cut it off, 'cos he was a fucking pervert!"

Kenny watched as the boy ran out of the room and heard heavy stomps up the stairs before a loud slam of a bedroom door.

Will coughed uncomfortably and leaned in towards Eric.

"I have to say that we will want to talk with Nate about what he has accused Jason of. It could help us track down whoever did this."

"Why? I can't believe that Jason would have been doing things like that." Eric had paled visibly as the thought of his own son being a molester finally started to dawn on him and, worse, that Jason had been abusing his younger brother in this very house without him realising.

"I've known you since we were kids, Eric, so I'm

telling you this off the record. It's terrible, but I think you should know. Whoever killed Jason did, erm, cut off his penis."

"Oh my God! Why?"

"I'm not saying that he was, but if he was molesting Nate and someone found out," Will paused. "Or worse, if he was molesting another boy and was discovered, cutting off his penis is a known technique for dealing with, and punishing, child sex offenders."

"Jesus. I need to talk to Nate."

"Eric, I'm going to have to report this to Social Services and we will need to take Nate into care until this is sorted out."

"I've just lost one son," Eric growled.

"I know, but we need to get the truth from Nate and, well, Janet's reaction could cause him to change his story, or not tell us anything at all."

"Fine!" Eric spat. "But I want to see him."

Kenny rocked back onto his haunches and smiled to himself. Looking up towards the heavens, he said a silent prayer. *At least I know that Nate is safe now, and Zachary. No-one will ever hurt Zachary like that.*

Creeping away from the house, Kenny entered his

home to the sound of the fight. Running up the stairs, he burst into Zachary's room and froze.

Zachary was crawled into a corner, his hands over his face, rocking back and forth as his body shook with sobs.

His father was on the floor, face down. Kenny could see the belt wrapped around his fist and drops of red on the metal buckle. He turned his father over and saw an angled imprint of a bruise already starting on his forehead. Kenny put his hand on his father's chest, which was moving up and down at a steady pace so he knew that his dad would be fine.

As he walked towards his brother, his foot kicked a heavy object. Looking down, Kenny saw the Spelling Bee trophy that Zachary had won the previous year. A small trickle of blood ran down one corner of the stone base.

"Hey, Zack," Kenny said softly, sitting next to his crying brother. "It's okay. I'm here." He turned his brother's face towards him and cringed as he saw the cut on Zachary's cheek. He pulled out his handkerchief and dabbed at it, cleaning away the red blood from his brother's tanned skin.

"Why does everyone hate me?" Zachary sobbed, trying to pull away.

"Not everyone," Kenny joked.

Zachary pushed Kenny away and scrambled to sit

on his bed. "You hate me for killing Mum. Dad hates me as well. No-one likes me. You all wish I was dead. Maybe it would have been better if I hadn't even been born!"

Kenny stepped back, shocked at the venom in his brother's voice. "Don't be stupid, retard," he said, jumping on the bed. Grabbing his brother, he started to tickle Zachary under his ribs, knowing that it would bring laughter.

Sure enough, within seconds, Zachary was a giggling mess and the younger boy looked up at Kenny with love in his eyes.

"Are we okay?" Kenny asked.

"Sure," Zachary smiled, leaning his head onto his older brother's shoulder. In a quiet voice, Zachary said, "Dad did upset Charlie though."

"Who's Charlie?" Kenny asked.

"Who?" Zachary replied.

"Charlie? You said Dad upset Charlie."

"Did I? I don't remember," Zachary said just as he yawned loudly, his mouth stretching fully open. "Can I sleep in with you tonight, just in case Dad tries to hit me again?"

Kenny had a strange feeling. All the hatred that he had been storing up against his brother for the twelve years since his mother's death vanished. He stared into Zachary's eyes and saw such pain that he felt tears swell in his own eyes. His breath caught in his throat.

Pulling Zachary close to him, he whispered into his brother's ear. "Of course, you can. I promise that I will never let Dad, Jason or anyone hurt you again. I swear to God, I will kill them all first."

"Jason can't hurt anyone ever again," Zachary yawned.

Zachary felt his body lift up as Kenny carried him into his bedroom. By the time that Kenny had changed into his own night-time t-shirt and shorts, Zachary was sleeping blissfully, a soft smile on his face. Kenny's heart expanded with love, and he dropped to his knees by the side of his bed.

"I swear to you now Zack," Kenny's voice was soft, quiet, confident. "No-one will ever hurt you again, even if I have to kill them dead," he paused, his thoughts going to his former friend. "As dead as Jason."

Chapter 6

May 2021

Zack and Paula walked back into the interview room. Dan was smiling broadly while Harry Gillespie looked a little uncomfortable. Sitting down opposite them, Zack leaned over to start the tape.

"Can we talk off the record for the moment?" Harry said.

Paula looked up, surprised at the nervous tone in his voice. "What is it that you want to say? Anything that is said off tape can't be used in court, other than in witness statements by DC Jacobs and myself."

"My client is willing to divulge certain pieces of information in exchange for immunity from any prosecution, along with guarantees of his safety."

Paula groaned. "Is this another one of your plays,

Harry, because I'm too stressed, tired and frankly fed up with all of the tricks that you pull."

"No," Harry said quietly. "But this could help you with your investigation. If we do not get that agreement, then I have no choice but to tell my client to refuse to reveal the identity of the woman who has been abusing him, along with further details of immoral actions that my client feels is instrumental to the death of his stepmother."

"You know that we can't agree to that in here, Harry." Paula paused. "And I will need something to take to the DI before he'd even consider something like this."

Zack sat up in his chair, knowing that it was his turn to play the so-called bad cop in the scenario.

"And it will need to be good, son," he said across the table, staring Dan straight in his eyes. "At the moment, we are picking apart your alibi, and with the assault on your uncle, and the alleged assault on your cousin ... well, I'm tempted to tell the DI to release your dad and hold you as the main suspect."

"FUCK OFF!" Dan spat. "I didn't kill Mary. Nor did Dad! It was him; I'm telling you." Harry stood and put his hands on the young boy's shoulders as he started to climb across the table.

"It was who, Dan?" Paula asked softly. "If you know who it was, tell us and we will make sure that they never get to you."

Dan slumped back in his chair. A tear trickled down his cheek, which he wiped away with his left hand.

"I dunno exactly," he sniffed. "But I'm pleased he did it."

"Why? What was she doing to you?" Zack asked, his tone reconciliatory. "Was it Mary who was abusing you?"

The façade that Dan had surrounded himself with, finally broke. "She made me do stuff. I didn't wanna but she threatened to tell Dad after the first time."

"Dan, maybe we should talk before you say any more?" Harry suggested, laying his hand on the boy's.

"No!" Dan snapped. "She hurt me, which is why I hurt others. I didn't mean to hurt Philip, but he wouldn't leave it alone."

"So, are you saying that Philip killed Mary?" Zack asked. He glanced across at Paula, a frown of disbelief on his face.

"Oh god no," Dan laughed. "Philip's a wimp and a nerd. He couldn't hurt a fly." Dan's face turned serious. "You've gotta protect me from him if I tell you. Otherwise, he'll chop me up. He said he would."

"I thought you said you didn't see him?" Zack pushed.

"I didn't," the boy whimpered. "But he knew I was there. He said that he'd done it to protect me."

"Who?" Paula asked. "Who is protecting you, Danny? Who are you protecting?"

"My … name … is … Dan …" the boy spat.

Zack looked into the eyes of the boy and saw a flat look of hatred. He put his hand on Paula's and motioned for them to leave.

"Harry, we are not going to charge your client with anything at this moment, but we will want to keep him as a material witness. We are holding the right to recall him for further questioning, should we need to, for help in continuing the investigation."

Zack leaned over and stopped the tape. "Where are you going to stay tonight?"

"I've arranged an overnight foster placement, for the short-term," Harry said quietly. "They'll look after him."

"Take care, Dan," Zack said as the two detectives turned to walk out.

"Detective Jacobs?" Dan's voice sounded small, afraid, weak.

Zack turned back to look at the boy and he felt his heart pull at the sight of the frightened child.

"Don't let Charlie get me, please."

"Who?" Zack felt a shiver run through him.

"I don't know who he is, but he scares me."

Zack and Paula watched as Harry led the young boy out of the room.

"Are you okay? You look like you've seen a ghost," Paula said.

"Where did this Charlie come from?" Zack asked, his hand shaking as he picked up the bottle of water that he had brought in for Dan. He concentrated on it as he lifted it to his mouth, taking a long drink from it.

"He's bullshitting again, Zack," Paula hissed. "Can't you see that? He knows we're on to him so he's diverting the attention."

"That's got to be it," Zack said, placing the bottle back down.

"Absolutely not!" DI Michaels snapped at Zack. "I am not letting you anywhere near that bastard."

"Boss, he knows me," Zack sat down heavily. "I can probably get more information out of him than anyone else."

"But it could also trigger memories for you." Will sighed. "There are things that you don't remember from what happened before, and I promised your dad that I'd protect you."

"My father is dead."

"Zack, you know what I mean …"

61

"I know. But Dan mentioned a name that we don't have on file. I honestly believe that he was telling the truth."

"Why?"

"I've seen kids lie to try to get out of things, and I've seen kids who are scared of parents or teachers. I looked him in the eyes and honestly believe that Dan is scared of this person who, he is claiming, killed Mary."

"So why will talking with Richard help?"

"He may know who this man is," Zack shrugged. "I've got a horrible feeling that Dan is in trouble and that this guy, Charlie, may come after him."

"You said Harry has arranged a placement tonight?"

"I've sent a couple of uniforms to sit outside."

"Then forget about it for tonight and go home. Get some sleep and we'll start again tomorrow."

"Okay Uncle Will."

"Maybe go see your dad … erm, Sammy."

Chapter 7

June 2000

"Come on," Ian moaned. "Why does he have to come along?"

"'Cos I've promised him I'll look after him!" Kenny snapped.

"But he's such a wuss," Peter whined.

Zachary stared down at his feet, kicking his left one against his right. He knew that Peter was right; he simply wasn't as rough and tumble as his older brother and his friends, but ever since Jason's murder, Kenny had insisted on keeping him close.

"I'm fine if you want me to go home," he offered.

"No," Kenny said a little harsher than he meant to, cringing inside as he saw his brother flinch. He walked over and put his arm around him.

"Awww, look at the brotherly love," George

sniggered.

"Don't any of you worry about the bloke who killed Jason?" Dicky asked, standing up for Kenny. "He's not been caught yet."

"Well, none of us are pervs so we'll be fine," Jack shrugged. "Come on, let's get a move on, or we'll miss the bus."

As a group, they turned down the darkened lane and ran towards the main street where the bus stop was located. Zachary panted as he tried to keep up with the older boys, but as they were all members of the school football team, he was soon being left behind.

"Guys … wait for me," he huffed in between breaths. He stopped and leaned against a lamppost, pulling an asthma inhaler from his pocket.

A shadow fell over him and he felt a shiver, despite the warm summer sun. A momentary panic rushed through him.

"Come on, fuckwit," Ian hissed at him. "Your brother may want you with us, but if you're gonna be a pain, just fuck off home."

"I'm sorry," Zachary said weakly. "I'll try to keep up, promise."

The pair set off at a fast trot and soon caught up with the rest of the boys who were waiting patiently at the bus stop.

"Finally!" George moaned. "Told you he was going to be a drag."

"Leave him be!" Kenny snarled.

"Or what?"

"Or else!"

"Calm down," Dicky stood in between the two boys who were squaring up to each other. "I'll make sure he doesn't get left behind."

Kenny nodded at his friend, while giving George an evil stare.

"Thank you," Zachary said quietly as they boarded the bus, taking a seat beside the older boy.

"I told you before," Dicky said. "I'll look after you."

Zachary gave him a small smile and sat looking out of the window at the shops as they whizzed by. He tried to ignore the banter from his brother's friends as they talked about which horror films were showing at the cinema, and which one would make the younger boy 'piss his pants'.

The bus finally arrived in town and the lads rushed off it, pushing and shoving each other playfully. They turned the corner.

"MACCIES!!!" They all shouted in unison.

"Ah man, I've not had a Big Mac in yonks," Ian said, rubbing his stomach.

"Damn" Peter whined. "I've only got enough for the cinema, and I thought we were getting popcorn in there."

Zachary walked up to the taller lad and pulled out a five pound note. "Here Peter," he said, putting the note into his hand. "I've been saving up for a special occasion, but this is, sort of. I've not been to watch a scary film before."

Peter stared at the younger boy, a mixture of feelings running through him. "I don't need your money," he said, shoving the boy. Zachary stumbled backwards, his feet slipping off the kerb.

"Zack!" Kenny yelled, trying to grab his younger brother but was too late. He watched as Zachary's head hit the road, the boy crying out in pain.

"What the fuck did you just do?" Kenny snarled and turned towards Peter, fists clenched, as Dicky rushed over to Zachary.

"The little snot nose tried to embarrass me!" Peter hissed.

"No, he didn't. He was trying to be nice."

"I'm okay, really," Zachary said as Dicky helped him back to his feet. Zachary rubbed the back of his head, feeling a bump forming, but was pleased that there was no blood. "Let's just go and watch the film."

With a nod of agreement from Kenny, the boys headed inside the foyer.

"Are you sure your cousin will let us in?" Jack asked Ian.

"'Course she will," Ian giggled. "She fancies Kenny so all he has to do is smile at her sweetly."

"Urgh," Zachary sniggered. "What? Girls are horrid!"

"Give it time, my young apprentice," Dicky laughed, poking the boy in the ribs, pleased to see a smile back on his face. "You'll grow to appreciate them."

Ignoring the finger in mouth gesture from his younger brother, Kenny gathered up the money from the boys and approached the counter. A momentary panic set in as he looked at the stern face of an elderly man before Ian's cousin opened up a second till. Rushing over to her, Kenny let loose his killer dimpled smile.

"Seven for Final Destination please."

"Are you old enough?" Karen Hollis asked with a faked frown upon her face. Well, she couldn't just let the boy have whatever he wanted, could she?

"Here is my ID," Kenny stammered, handing across a folded piece of paper. He hoped that Ian hadn't been lying and that she did fancy him.

Karen smiled as she opened the paper and saw a phone number written inside. She hit the button and seven tickets popped out. "That'll be £30.80 please, my love."

Kenny felt a warm glow spread through him as the girl mouthed that she would call him, and he grabbed the tickets. Turning back to the group of waiting boys, he strutted over to them like the alpha male that he knew he was.

Ignoring the ribbing from them, Kenny led the way to the screen, Ian and Peter pestering him for information. George, Jack and Richard followed them, with Zachary tagging along behind.

"I need the toilet," Zachary said as soon as they were seated in the darkened cinema.

"It's not even started yet, and he wants to piss!" Ian giggled.

"God, give it a rest, will you!" Kenny groaned.

"I need to go as well," George announced. "Come on squirt, I'll take you."

Kenny gave him a nod of thanks and watched his brother led away by his friend. The lights darkened even further, and the opening adverts came on.

In the lobby, Zachary looked around for the toilet and was pushed forward by George.

"It's over there," the older boy said, a hint of annoyance in his voice. "I've been looking forward to this movie, so don't make us late!"

"Okay, okay," Zachary said, and followed George into the toilet. There was a row of a dozen urinals, with three men already spread down the line. George guided the boy to the low urinal, sniggering to himself that he was reminding Zachary that he wasn't really part of their gang, just the younger hanger oner. Zachary frowned, unzipped and sighed with relief as the stream of urine splattered against the blue chemical blocks that were in the urinals.

"Ah man, that feels good!" George chuckled. He glanced down unconsciously and saw that Zachary had already finished, but was stood still, waiting to zip up. "What? You need my permission to shake? Or are you wishing that I was a perv like Jason? I've got news for you … I'm not, and no one is going to fiddle with a little snotty shit like you."

Zachary blushed. He hadn't realised that he'd finished and had been staring at the wall. Tucking himself away, he zipped up and rushed over to wash his hands.

George shouldered into him. "Come on … I don't want to miss the start," he growled at the boy. "Let's go."

"Aren't you going to wash your hands?"

"Why? Your's might be diseased, but my dick is clean."

Zachary frowned but followed George out of the toilets and they quickly retook their seats. Zachary was pleased that he was next to Kenny and Dicky. They both asked if he was okay, and if George had given him *any shit* in the toilet. He shrugged.

After the film, they waited patiently for the bus as the rain hammered down. Zachary shivered, his light t-shirt offering no resistance to the downpour. He tried to squeeze under the small bus shelter but was pushed back out by George. Once again, his trainers betrayed him and he slipped over, managing to save his head but landing heavily on his elbows. Holding back sniffles, Zachary scrambled to his feet before anyone could have the chance to help. He didn't want to be the weak kid, the hanger on. He didn't want Kenny or Dicky to have to stand up for him.

Shooting a look at the older boy, Zachary moved under the shelter into the space that an elderly lady had left when she got onto her bus. Sitting down on the seat, dark thoughts started running through his head.

"What are you thinking about, squirt?" Kenny asked, nudging his brother to make sure he was okay from his latest fall.

"Just that it would be great if George did what Terry did in the film, and got hit by a bus," Zachary replied, a low tone in his voice.

Kenny looked down and saw a steely glint to his brother's eyes but shrugged it off. After all, George had picked on his brother twice that night, three times, if he counted the incident in the toilet which George had bragged about.

One by one, the boys got off the bus at their various stops until it was just George, Kenny and Zachary left. George was one stop beyond the Downes' boys, and they said their goodbyes.

Walking through the front door, Zachary immediately stiffened.

"What's up?"

"Dad's been drinking again," the young boy whimpered.

"Don't worry," Kenny said. "He'll not hurt you. Not tonight. I promise. Go to bed and let me worry about what Dad is doing."

Zachary quickly ran upstairs and closed his bedroom door as Kenny walked into the lounge to talk to his father.

"Zack! Zack! Are you awake?"

"Huh?" Zachary rubbed his eyes. He was lying on top of his bed, still dressed from the trip to cinema. How had he fallen asleep in his wet clothes? His dad would never believe that he hadn't wet the bed, and that it was just his rain-soaked clothes.

"Come on, Zack, open the door!" Kenny's voice sounded panicked.

He dragged himself to his feet, pulling off the wet clothes and grabbing a pair of underpants to slip on to hide his modesty. Opening the door, he stared at his rain-soaked brother.

"Where have you been?"

"I've been here on my bed?" Zachary moaned. "You've just woken me up."

"You wouldn't answer earlier, Dad's been out looking for you, and I went out looking as well." The older brother's eyes had a hard edge to them. "You need to stop sleepwalking, especially now."

"Why now?" Zachary asked, confused.

"That bloke has struck again."

"What bloke?"

"Jason's killer. Only this time, it's George. Someone has chopped up George."

Chapter 8

May 2021

"You know I could get into a whole heap of shit for this, Zack," Lawrence Williams said.

Zack's eyes pleaded with the desk sergeant. "Come on Lawrie," he started. "I'll owe you one."

"You'll owe me several for this." Lawrence said as he picked up the keys to the holding cells. "This will break just about every regulation that we have, especially with no solicitor here!"

"Look, if he doesn't want to talk, then I won't force it. I'll leave," Zack said. "But I'm hoping that he will and that he can help us to help his son."

"His son is that Dan kid you were talking to earlier?" Lawrence's face had taken a stern expression.

"Yeah ... you checked him in and out, didn't you?"

"Not passing any judgement, Zack," the sergeant paused. "But he's a little shit. Him and his friends have been bullying my little nephew. I went up the school to talk to the principal, but he didn't seem to give a crap about it."

"Off the record, Lawrie," Zack said quietly. "Dan has admitted to being a bully, but it is a reaction to the abuse that he has been suffering."

"Bullshit … nothing makes a kid get a gang of his mates to break the fingers of an eleven year old."

"What?"

"Oliver, my nephew, plays the piano. He's really good at it, and there was talk about him being fast tracked into the Symphony Orchestra. Your precious victim and his friends snapped every finger on both of his hands. The doctors don't know if they will ever heal well enough for him to play again, let alone at the standard that he was."

Zack could feel the anger rolling from Lawrence.

"Oli tried to hang himself, but my sister walked in on him. He is on medication now."

"I'm so sorry," Zack said, putting his arm on his colleague's shoulder. "Dan actually did that?"

"Dan was there, but it was one of his gang of thugs, Marc Wood, that actually did the breaking. I swear, if I ever catch him alone …"

"Let's not go there," Zack said. "I know it's tough, but things will work out."

They walked in silence down the brightly lit corridor that had metal cell doors on each side. Lawrence stopped outside a door about halfway down and put the key in the lock. He flipped open the small metal plate that served as a viewing slot into the cell.

"Okay Hopkins, stand away from the door, back against the far wall. You know the drill," Lawrence said and there was sound of movement from inside the cell.

Lawrence turned the key and opened the door, stepping into the doorway, his frame filling the entryway.

"I have a Detective Jacobs who wants to ask you some questions," he started. "But you are under no pressure to have to talk to him without your solicitor present."

"Who's Detective Jacobs?" Richard asked meekly.

Zack stepped into view. Memories flooded back to him of the bullying that his brother's friends had subjected him to, and, for a moment, his hands clenched into fists.

"Zack," Richard started, a look of surprise on his face. "Is that you?"

"Richard," Zack acknowledged, nodding his head at him.

"I'd heard you had become a cop, but wow, a detective. Well done."

"Richard, I'm not here for a catch up or to exchange pleasantries," Zack said softly. "I'm on the team investigating Mary's death."

Richard stiffened slightly before sighing and sitting down on the hard, blue mattress that lay on top of the bed.

"Now, as Sergeant Williams said, you don't have to talk to me without your lawyer being here …"

"No, it's fine," Richard said. "Unless you've changed dramatically from when you were younger, I trust you."

Zack looked over at Lawrence and nodded.

"Let me know when you're finished," Lawrence said.

The door closed behind the Sergeant, and the click of the lock sounded before the echoes of footsteps faded away down the hallway.

Zack took a seat next to Richard, looking into his eyes.

"I've been talking with Dan and, while I can't say too much," Zack paused. "I don't really know how to ask you this."

"I know what she was doing to him." Richard's eyes welled up with tears. "But I thought that he was enjoying it. He always gave it the 'big I am' whenever I tried to talk to him about girls, and well, about life in general."

"But he's underage," Zack hissed. "How could you let this go on?"

"Our marriage had broken down; she was the money earner. Her family is rich, and it was about three years into our marriage that the problems started. She was drinking far too much. Wine mainly, but I found bottles of vodka scattered around the house in various hiding places."

"So, she was an alcoholic," Zack stated rather than asked. "Dan did say something like that."

"She was a drunk, and a mean one as well." Richard rolled up his shirt. Various scars littered his chest and sides. "Her responses to me trying to stop her drinking, and then stop her from taking Dan was always the same. I'd wake up in the middle of the night with a fresh cut from a knife where she had decided to punish me."

"Look mate," Zack sighed, sympathy starting to flow from him for the lad who had protected him from the other bullies. "I shouldn't be saying this, but you have a great case for a self-defence claim, especially playing on her abuse of Dan."

"I don't want Dan involved in this," Richard spat. "It's why I turned myself in. I let him down, just like I let you and the others down when we were kids."

Zack paused, his mind playing through the sudden scenario that had crashed into his thoughts.

"Richard, you can't take the fall if you're innocent."

"I can, and I will, if it saves Dan."

"I don't think Dan did this either," Zack said. "I think there was someone else there, and you covering for Dan will muddy any investigation into this."

"Who could have been there? I was on my way home from work. I'd had a call that Dan was skipping school again. Could it have been one of his friends?"

"I'm not sure, but my gut is screaming at me that Dan didn't do this."

"I know that my lad isn't the most pleasant of boys," Richard sighed. "I have been called to the school, I don't know how many times, about him bullying others or getting into fights, which is partly why I left this thing with Mary alone. I thought that if it was a pleasurable thing that he was enjoying, then it might make him stop with the aggression but, looking back, it only made things worse."

"I am going to need the names of his friends, the ones that you think could be involved with the bullying."

"Of course," Richard said. "Dan would hang around with his best friend, Henry Lavery, Henry's girlfriend Libby Forrest, Marc Wood, Tony Gwynne, and his cousin Philip, although Philip's not a blood cousin, I guess. He is Mary's nephew."

"What about someone called Charlie?"

"Who?"

"Dan mentioned a Charlie, who may have been at the scene. He seemed scared of him."

"I don't know any of his friends called that," Richard apologised. "Sorry."

"You've been helpful enough for now," Zack said standing up. "I'm going to see if I can get you released, but you have to stop saying that you did this."

"Thanks Zack," Richard stood and offered his hand, which Zack took. "You were always a good kid."

"If you remember anything else, anything that can help, please let me know."

Zack rapped on the door and, within moments, the key turned, quickly followed by the scrape of the door opening.

"Take care Richard."

As Lawrence and Zack walked back to the desk, the duty Sergeant turned to the detective.

"So, what did he have to say?"

"He's innocent, he's trying to protect his son."

"Figured as much. I have seen him at parent teacher meetings. I thought that something really bad must have happened for him to have murdered her in such a way. It would have been so out of character for him. Now, that lad of his and the lad's friends, that's something else."

Zack grunted, running through the list of names that Richard had given him. "I think I may need to have a chat with some of these."

Chapter 9

June 2000

Sammy Jacobs took a deep breath as he gripped the handle of the door to the classroom. He had a sinking feeling in his gut that the class was not going to take the news well and, to be honest, he couldn't blame them.

Opening the door, he was greeted with the usual cacophony of noise from the twelve year olds. It was a mix of laughter and joking, of chatter and shouting. He picked up a snippet about how badly England had played the night before, losing to Portugal after being 2-0 up.

He strode purposefully to his desk at the front of the class and put his rucksack on the top, besides a neat pile of exercise books.

At least they remembered to do their homework, Sammy mused. He scanned the classroom, noting that all of his form were in attendance. His heart felt for Jessica Brown, who was a pupil short this morning.

"Okay, settle down people," he said, knowing that it would take a few attempts to get them to quieten down. It always did after a big football match, especially when it was the national team in a major tournament.

His eyes caught those of Zachary Downes, the only pupil in the class who was sitting quietly, ignoring the prodding of his fellow classmate Bobby Hemmings. Bobby was a livewire, always the joker, always wanting to be the centre of attention, whereas Zachary was, in Sammy's eyes, the perfect student. Polite, courteous, solid B grades verging on A's. Sammy had longed for a relationship with someone, anyone, so that he could fulfil his dream of being a father to a son, but it had never happened, so he had thrown himself into looking after his students. Zachary was the epitome of what he had dreamed to be his perfect son.

"Okay class, settle down," he said, raising his voice above the noise of the class. "Settle down, come on people."

Zachary looked at Bobby; an involuntary nod stopped his friend's inane chatter.

"What's wrong?" Bobby asked his friend.

"Mr Jacobs is going to tell everyone about George," Zachary replied sadly.

"George?"

"George Adams, Kenny's mate."

"What about him?"

"He's dead."

"WHAT? What do you mean he's dead?" Bobby's voice went up two octaves, blasting over the background chatter, causing the class to fall silent and stare at the pair.

"Settle down!" Sammy said, a little harsher than he meant. The class turned to stare at him, eyes wide as they tried to digest Bobby's statement.

Sammy walked to the front of his desk and perched on it, rocking back and forth slightly. He rubbed his thumb and forefinger across the bridge of his nose before looking at each of his pupils.

"It pains me to have to tell you that, yesterday, the police found the body of George Adams in the woods. It appears that he is a victim of the same person who killed Jason Billings."

The classroom erupted. Sounds of panic and tears rang around the room, and Sammy could hear similar outbursts from the adjoining classrooms.

"Listen, you are not in any danger here," Sammy tried to reassure them. "So, let's take a breath and listen to what I need to tell you."

"Sir?" A girl with blonde locks started. "Is it a serial killer? Are we all going to die?"

"Tracy, we don't know that it's, um, that," Sammy said, not wanting to say the words. "But the police are bringing in some rules that we all need to follow, which is what I want to talk to you about."

"Was George a pervert like Billings?" Bobby asked. "Is that why he's been killed?"

"What do you mean, a pervert?" Freddie Kenton said. "The only pervert here is him." He threw a scrunched-up piece of paper at Zachary who batted it away.

"Fuck you," Bobby stood up. "You know that Jason was fiddling with Nate, don't you? Nate was supposed to be your mate."

"Nate's a fag," Freddie shot back.

"You take that back," Zachary said, his voice dropping to a chilling whisper.

Bobby looked at his friend and, for a moment, did not recognise him. Zachary's eyes, normally a brilliant blue, had turned into a flat, grey stare. His mouth, with his ready smile, was just a thin line of pale pink lips. Zachary's clenched knuckles were white with tension.

"Zack," Bobby said quietly. "Zack, come on mate, calm down."

Sammy watched as the boy seemed to shake himself from a daze; the blue eyes returning as he glanced around the room, seemingly to restore his consciousness to the present.

"Fucking weirdo," Freddie muttered under his breath.

"Settle down, now!" Sammy said, raising his voice to a tone that the students knew would stand for no more trouble. "Freddie, you've earned yourself a nice stay after school in detention."

"Aw man," the stocky lad hissed, shooting a look at Zachary. He drew his finger across his neck in a slicing movement.

Sammy stood and walked around his desk to the dark green chalk board. Picking up a white stick, he wrote "6.30PM" in large letters.

"Detective Michaels has asked all the schools, with the mayor's blessing, to introduce a curfew, starting tonight. No child under the age of sixteen will be allowed out of their home without parental supervision after six thirty pm."

Cries of disbelief and shouts of "no way" rang around the classroom. Sammy picked up a heavy textbook and slammed it onto the top of his desk. The thud silenced the room.

"Look kids, I know it sounds harsh and draconian," he paused. "Look that word up, and I want it in a five-hundred-word story tomorrow."

More moans from the class.

"Until the police catch the person who is responsible for these horrific crimes, we all think it is best that we take precautions. I know that we have done the stranger danger talk in the past," he started.

"Tell that to the perv," Freddie hissed.

"But this is serious. Two of our pupils, two of your friends have been killed. Until we get the son of a bitch ..." a brief snigger from the back of the class did not phase Sammy. "Until we know that you are all going to be okay, then we have to make sure that no child is in unnecessary danger again."

A ringing bell announced the end of the registration period and three quarters of the students stood to make their way to the first lesson of the day. Bobby stood up to leave for his first lesson, raised his fist and bumped it with Zachary who remained in his seat, his first lesson being English Literature taught by Mr Jacobs.

As Freddie Kenton walked past his desk, Zachary felt a shove and his books spilled over onto the floor.

"See you later Downsey!" the boy hissed at him. "You're gonna regret getting me detention."

"So, who can tell me what the true moral of the story is?" Sammy asked his class, holding up the book in front of them. "Why did Romeo want to kill himself?"

His students looked back at him, the silence

deafening. It was always a difficult topic. Shakespeare could be considered very dry, but it was expected reading. Sammy looked around the room and his eyes settled once again on Zachary.

"Romeo was an idiot," the young boy said. "He thought that love was everything and couldn't imagine life without it."

"And who falls in love so quickly?" Tracy Smith added. "It's stupid that someone would kill themselves over someone they only met three days earlier!"

The class broke into several discussion groups and Sammy watched them with interest. Each group were raising valid points and he was pleased that the students had moved on from their initial anger at the announcement of the curfew.

Eventually the bell sounded, signalling the end of the lesson and the students quickly stuffed books and pens into their bags and scrambled to head outside for the morning break.

"Zachary, can you stay back for a second," Sammy asked.

The boy waited in his seat as the class filed out. "What's up, sir?" he asked politely.

"How are you?" Sammy said, walking over and taking the seat in front of the boy. He sat backwards on the chair, his legs around the back so that he was facing Zachary whilst still giving him distance.

"I'm fine, sir," Zachary replied. "Why are you asking?"

"I know that you were friends with both boys."

"They were friends of Kenny's, not mine."

Sammy heard the hardening of the boy's voice and his stare seemed flat, almost zombielike.

"What I mean is ..."

"I'm fine." He said in the same level tone. "I need to go and get some air."

The boy stood up and, without waiting for a response from his teacher, left the room.

"Something isn't quite right there," Sammy mused to himself and made a vow to keep an eye on the lad.

Zachary rubbed his eyes as he found himself walking along the corridor. He paused for a moment before pushing open the door that led to the playground. He couldn't remember leaving the classroom but all thoughts of that left his head as he felt his arms grabbed. He was spun around and pushed heavily through the door. He felt a stinging pain as his hand scraped against the brick wall as he stumbled back into a standing position. A fist connected with his stomach and the air whooshed out of his lungs as he doubled over in pain.

Fists and kicks rained in on the boy as he rolled himself into a ball to try to protect his body.

"Told you I'd get you, Downsey," Freddie hissed at him before aiming a kick at Zachary's face.

There was a crunch as Zachary felt his nose split open and he tasted blood in his mouth. His mind reeled and he felt lightheaded. He could almost feel himself floating away from his body and he closed his eyes, praying that the pain would end.

He opened his eyes as he felt no kicks or punches and was surprised to find himself standing up. He was rubbing his right hand and glanced down. His knuckles were grazed and there were smears of red on them.

I must have rubbed my nose, he thought to himself before he saw the three squirming bodies on the floor in front of him. Sobs were coming from all three.

"Freddie?" Zachary started and moved towards the boy who had led the attack on him.

"Leave me alone," Freddie cried out, struggling to his feet to get away from the boy. "You're fucking crazy!"

Freddie helped his two friends up and the three scrambled away, tripping over several times before rounding the corner of the building, disappearing from sight.

There was a noise behind Zachary, a scraping of

shoes in the gravel and he turned around, raising his fists to defend himself from another attack.

"Bloody hell, Zack," Bobby said, rushing over to his friend. "Your nose is a mess, but Jesus … I never knew you could fight like that."

"Fight like what?"

"They were kicking you and I was going to go and get Mr Jacobs, but then you suddenly managed to get up and you fought them like you were possessed or something." Bobby had a look of awe in his eyes. "You didn't seem to feel their punches and you downed all three of them with a couple of punches each. Then you were punching Freddie until he started crying."

"I don't remember," Zachary said, still rubbing his right hand.

The bell rang, signalling the end of the break and they headed back inside, Zachary dabbing at his bloody nose with his handkerchief.

Chapter 10

May 2021

"There he is," Marc Wood hissed as he leaned against the school gates. "That's the fucking snitch."

Libby Forrest turned her lip up as she spied a small boy leaving the school. "He is so up himself, the little prick." She brushed the brown lock of hair out of her eyes and nudged her boyfriend who was standing next to her, absently smoking on a stolen cigarette.

"Watch it, Libs," Henry Lavery complained as he bent down to retrieve the cigarette that she had knocked from his hand. "I've only got another two of these."

"You know I don't like the taste of them on you," she complained.

"Where's Tony and Dan?" Marc said softly, his

eyes never leaving the young boy, who was glancing around as if looking for someone.

"Dan is still with the police," Henry said.

"I heard Tony got a detention from Mr Harrison," Libby added. "He tripped Williams up in the corridor and Harrison saw him."

Marc grabbed the cigarette from Henry, took in one long drag and threw it onto the floor, stubbing it out with his foot. Releasing the inhaled smoke in one long breath, he said, "fine. We'll do this without them."

Ignoring the muttered complaints from Henry, Marc started to head in the direction of the young boy.

Oliver Williams sensed the approach of the three older students before he saw them. His stomach flipped over, and he looked around. Spotting an alleyway that led to Spring Road, his panicked mind decided on flight rather than staying in what could be safety in numbers around the school gates.

"Get back here, you little snitch," Marc shouted as he saw the boy take off.

The three of them started running after the younger boy, their school bags slung over their shoulders.

"The little bastard can run fast," Henry gasped. He was the slowest of the three, something that his girlfriend liked to remind him of.

"I'll get him, don't worry," Libby chuckled. She stopped for a moment, took her school bag off and handed it to her boyfriend, before taking off after the fleeing target.

"You really need to get fit, mate," Marc sniggered as the pair of boys slowly walked in the direction of the speeding girl.

"Fuck off," Henry pushed him back. "At least I've got a girlfriend."

"I don't need a steady one," Marc shot. He stretched his lithe frame. "I have all of the girls wanting this," he said, indicating his own physique.

In the distance, they heard a high-pitched yell. They sniggered to each other and started jogging towards the shouting.

As they turned the corner onto Spring Road, they saw Libby kneeling on the fallen boy. Every slap to his face was punctuated with her words, and his yelps.

"I." Libby slapped the boy's face.

"Ow." Oliver cried.

"Told."

"Ow."

"You."

"Please."

"Not."

"Ow."

"To."

"Help."

"Run."

"Ow."

Marc looked down at Oliver and saw blood streaming from a cut on his forehead and he glanced at Libby.

"He hit his head on the kerb when I tripped him," she shrugged.

Marc slowly walked up to the boy. He stepped onto his left wrist, pinning his arm to the ground. He could see the slightly misshapen fingers, remnants of their previous encounter.

"What did I tell you when we last had this conversation?" Marc hissed, his voice deadly and low.

"I didn't tell anyone," Oliver whimpered. "Honest."

"If you didn't tell, then why was I suspended?" Marc hocked up in his throat and spat into the boy's face.

Oliver cringed as he felt the saliva dribbled down his cheek. He wanted to answer, but also wanted to keep his mouth closed for fear of the spit seeping into his mouth.

He cried out as Libby slapped his face, her hand stinging across his cheek.

"I don't know," Oliver cried. "Someone must have seen and told. It wasn't me, you've gotta believe me."

"Why should I believe a snot nosed little brat like you?" the girl sneered.

"Just kick him in and let's go," Henry said. "I've gotta go visit my Nanna."

Marc sniggered at him before turning his attention back to the prone boy.

"Now listen here," he said. "You leave my sister alone, don't even speak to her. You ever tell anyone on us again, and it will be more than your fingers that we break next time."

Oliver nodded fearfully, trying desperately not to let the situation get the better of his bladder that was threatening to embarrass him. Marc turned away for a second before turning back. Oliver screamed as the boy slammed his foot onto his pinned hand and he felt fingers that were still healing break once more.

"Ew!" Libby said, jumping off the boy as dampness spread across the grey school trousers. She pulled out her phone and took a couple of quick photos. "You tell anyone, and these pictures will be everywhere."

Their laughter was interrupted by a shout from across the road.

"What are you kids doing?" An old lady was crossing the road towards them.

"Piss off Granny!" Marc laughed and they turned and ran back down the alleyway, making their escape.

Zack and Bobby walked into Bristol Royal Infirmary. The smell of hygiene was evident as the country still battled with the Covid-19 pandemic. Bobby fiddled with the surgical mask that was required to be worn at every hospital as they walked up to the reception desk. Taking their ID badges out, Zack approached the weary looking middle-aged lady behind the counter.

"DC Jacobs and PC Hemmings to see Oliver Williams," Zack said as way of introduction.

"Hold on one moment," she said. Taping away at her computer, a frown crept across her face. "He is still in with the doctor at the moment so if you wouldn't mind taking a seat."

They looked around at the empty waiting room, another symptom of the pandemic and took a seat. Bobby fetched them both a cup of water and they sipped as they contemplated this incident.

"You said this is Lawrence's nephew?" Bobby asked.

"Yeah," Zack sighed. "He's had his fingers broken before and one of Dan Hopkins' gang had done it."

"You think it's the same lad?"

"That's what we are here to find out. If it is, and we can get Oliver to confirm it, then this time, the boss wants us to be able to get enough evidence for CPS to press charges."

"I've never seen DI Michaels so upset."

"Well, it's a member of our family that's been attacked, again." Zack shook his head. He felt his vision blur slightly at the thought of the young boy prodigy being attacked for a second time.

"Wow Zack, I know this is horrible, but come on mate," Bobby had backed up slightly. "CPS can only prosecute with the right evidence."

"Huh?"

"You can't blame them for not being able to proceed without Oliver's statement, and the kid was obviously scared shitless of them."

"What do you mean?"

"Have you just blanked again?" Bobby asked, concern showing on his face. "You were just slating CPS something chronic."

"I felt a little dizzy but I'm fine," Zack lied. "But yeah, they really should have investigated it more." He glanced up to see if his ad-lib had worked and was pleased to see that Bobby had taken his comment as back up to whatever he had just said during the dizzy spell.

"Well, it looks like a Big Mac on the way back to the station," Bobby joked. "Why is it McDonalds that always seems to sort you out?"

"Oh, come on," Zack smiled. "I'm loving it!"

Bobby groaned just as they heard a scream from around the corner. They jumped up and made their way towards the sound but were stopped by an orderly.

"You can't go back there."

They flashed their badges and he begrudgingly moved to one side. They walked to a curtained area just as a young man in a long white coat came out. He had a pained expression on his face. Another voice from behind the curtain spoke in a soothing tone.

"It's over now Oli," the deep male voice said. "All of the dislocations are back in place. We will just need to splint up the breaks and you will be good to go."

The owner of the voice pulled back the curtain and stopped at the sight of the two men. Bobby was in his uniform and the doctor sighed. "I assume you are here to talk to Oliver, but I want to get the splints in place to stabilise the fractures as soon as possible."

"That's fine, doctor," Zack said, moving out of his

way. "We want the boy to be treated to the best of your abilities. He's one of ours."

They retook their seats and, after twenty minutes, the doctor returned. "Okay, you can speak with him now, but he is a little groggy. I had to give him some morphine for the pain that he was in."

Zack could hear the underlying anger in the man's voice and inclined his head.

"I treated Oliver the last time this happened. If this is the same boy, God help me, if I get my hands on him …"

"Don't worry Doc," Bobby said. "We'll make sure that the boy is punished this time."

They walked around to the treatment cubicle and Zack's heart sank as he saw Oliver's face streaked with tears. *How could anyone hurt a child like this?* he wondered.

"Maybe I should talk to him alone," Zack said. "Seeing a uniform may scare him."

Bobby nodded and stood to one side, as if guarding the cubicle.

"Hey Oli," Zack started. "I'm Zack. I'm a friend of your Uncle Lawrence."

"You're a police officer?" Oliver asked weakly.

"I am, and even better than that," he fished out his ID badge. "I'm a detective. Do you know what that is?"

"I'm not stupid," Oliver gave him a look of disdain. "I watch telly!"

"Sorry," Zack smiled. "What I meant was, it is my job to find people who have done bad things and catch them after the event."

"I'm not telling you who did this," Oliver shook his head.

"That's okay. I assumed that Marc would threaten you if you did tell."

"Yeah," Oliver replied before looking horrified. "I didn't say it was Marc."

"That's fine. Don't worry about it," Zack said, briefly touching the boy's shoulder in comfort. "Can you remember Mrs Roberts?"

"Who's she?"

"Mrs Roberts is the lady who shouted at them and then called the ambulance."

"Oh, the old lady," Oliver smiled remembering the kind words that the lady had said to him as she held his good hand and comforted him.

"Well, I showed her some photos and she identified Marc, Libby and Henry."

"So, you don't need me to tell you anything?" Oliver asked. "But they won't believe that I didn't."

"All I really need for you to tell me is why do you

think that they are picking on you and hurting you?"

"I live over the road from Marc and, last year, I asked Lucy out."

"Lucy?"

"His sister. She's real pretty, in my year and in the school orchestra. Marc has been hitting me ever since."

"So, when he broke your fingers last time, it was to stop you being in the orchestra and spending time with her?"

"I guess."

"So, why do you think he chased you today?"

"Lucy sat with me at lunch. I guess he must have seen it."

"Okay. Thank you, Oliver. Is someone coming to pick you up?"

There was movement behind them.

"Bloody hell. I'll kill the little shit."

"Uncle Lawrence!" Oliver said, his face brightening.

"Was it him again?"

Zack put a hand on the arm of the angry officer.

"It looks that way," he said. "But don't worry. We should have enough evidence this time to get CPS to do something."

"Bloody CPS!"

"Trust me, he won't get away with this."

Marc Wood was whistling to himself as he walked through the thick copse of trees. He was smiling as he thought back to the earlier events of the day. That little brat Williams needed to be taught to stay away from his precious little sister. No-one was allowed to kiss her. No-one!

He leaned against a tree and fished out the packet of Silk Cut that he swiped from his mother's purse. Pulling out a cigarette, he lit one up and took two long drags, revelling in the feeling of the smoke inside his lungs, the nicotine rush, before exhaling, trying to blow smoke rings, and groaning as his attempts failed once again.

There was a snap of a twig close by.

"Hello?" Marc said, dropping the cigarette and stubbing it out with his foot. He kicked some leaves over it, hiding the evidence. The last thing he wanted was another belting from his father.

There was no reply, just the chirping of whatever birds lived in the small wood that backed onto the family garden.

Marc frowned and contemplated trying to rescue the half-smoked nub when he heard another snap.

"Is that you Libby? Tony? Come on, stop pissing around!"

Silence greeted him. He could hear his own breath as the birds seemed to quieten down.

Another rustle of leaves and Marc spun to his left, his eyes widening as he saw a large figure looming towards him.

"Who the fuck? What the fuck?"

Marc felt pain explode in his brain as his body was hit with a heavy wooden handle. He struggled to catch his breath as the air in his lungs whooshed out.

"Who are you? What do you want?" the boy gasped before crying out as the end of the handle was thrust into his stomach.

The boy dropped to the ground; his hands spread in front of him. Shrieks filled the quiet forest air as the flat edge of a metal axe smashed into his fingers, breaking them.

Marc pulled up a hand, staring blankly at the mangled fingers before the pain overrode the shock induced adrenaline, and he sobbed.

"Who are you?"

"Charlie says you've been a naughty boy."

Marc saw light glint off the polished steel of the axe blade before it fell.

Chapter 11

June 2000

Bobby and Zachary walked slowly down the corridor, back towards the form room.

"Mate, your nose is a mess," Bobby frowned. "You should go to the nurse."

"I'll be fine," Zachary said. "Look, it's stopped bleeding." He offered his bloodied handkerchief to his friend who recoiled in mock horror.

"Keep your diseased ridden cloth away from me, you zombie freak!"

They reached the door and paused. Bobby looked through. "Freddie isn't in there," he reassured Zachary.

"Mr Jacobs is going to want to know where he is."

"That's his problem."

Bobby pushed Zachary through the door, before

they took their seats.

"Are you okay, Zack?" Tracy Smith asked, coming over to his desk. "Have you been in a fight?"

She took out a tissue and started to wipe Zachary's face, who squirmed away from her touch.

"Sit still," she said. "If Mr Jacobs sees you like this, he's going to want to know what happened."

The noise of the door closing startled them.

"What has happened, Mr Downes?" Sammy Jacobs asked.

"I tripped over at break, sir," Zachary said, not exactly lying.

"That looks pretty bad," Sammy said, his teacher instinct kicking in. "Have you seen the nurse?"

"Nah … it's fine now," Zachary replied. "It's stopped bleeding anyway."

"Why don't you nip to the bathroom and get cleaned up. I'll mark you as present and you can go onto your next class when the bell rings."

Zachary fist bumped Bobby, flashed a grateful smile at Tracy before leaving the classroom to the sound of Mr Jacobs asking where Freddie Kenton was.

As he pushed open the door to the boys' toilet, he heard angry muttering coming from inside. He held back to see what was happening.

"He did what? I thought that you were supposed to be a tough guy, but I guess I'll need to give you another lesson."

"Peter, don't." Freddie's voice sounded panicky before Zachary heard a grunt.

"I taught you to fight better, and you let a little shit like Zachary Downes beat you up."

There was another grunt and a yelp of pain.

"Peter, it was like he was mad or possessed or something. He took out me and Carl and Neil easily. He's supposed to be a wimp."

"You're the bloody wimp," Peter hissed at his younger brother. A slap echoed in the toilet. "I guess that I'm going to have to do your dirty work for you."

Zachary closed the door quietly and headed down the corridor to the toilet that was in the science block. Pushing the door open cautiously, he was relieved that this one was empty.

Walking up to the basin, he looked into the mirror. He grimaced at the amount of blood that was on his face and quickly grabbed some tissues from one of the stalls and wet them under the faucet. Dabbing at his face, he cleaned off the crimson evidence of the fight.

The fight.

Zachary could barely remember any details of it. Bobby was right. He must have been possessed or something. He remembered curling into a ball to protect his vitals from being kicked and yet, somehow, despite what Peter was calling his younger brother, he had managed to take down the toughest kid in his school year.

That's 'cos you're not a scaredy cat.

Zachary looked around to see who had come in and spoken but there was no one there. He shrugged. *I must be going mental like Bobby said.*

All other thoughts were banished as the shrill of the bell rang out, signifying the start of the next lesson. He headed out towards the biology lab and the prospect of a frog dissection.

Tracy Smith smiled as she saw Zachary walk into the lab. They had been sort of friends for some time, and she had had a crush on him since they were eight. He had always been quiet, nice and polite. However, he had always seemed to misinterpret her subtle signals that she wanted to be his girlfriend.

She had decided on a more assertive tactic. When she had seen the bloodied face, she had immediately taken her chance, helping him to clean up before Mr Jacobs had arrived, stopping her.

Now, in biology, she had a chance to investigate further, as Zachary was her lab partner, something that she had conspired with Philippa Higgins, who was only too pleased to swap seats so that Philippa was next to her own crush, Freddie Kenton.

Zachary smiled a sweet hello as he took his seat next to Tracy.

"So, what happened? Did you and Freddie have a fight?"

"I don't want to talk about it," Zachary replied softly. His eyes had a pained look in them.

"But if you did and you won, that makes you the toughest kid in the year."

Zachary was about to reply when Freddie walked into the class. There was a collective gasp from the students as they took in his dishevelled appearance, his bloodied shirt, the bruises already showing on his face.

He studiously avoided looking in the direction of Zachary and took his seat next to Philippa, who immediately started to fuss over him. It was a known fact that she wanted to be his girlfriend and, for once, he didn't seem to mind her attention.

Zachary's heart ached slightly for the lad, as he knew now that Freddie's older brother Peter was bullying him, just like Kenny had been doing to him.

He was about to stand and go over to Freddie when the door opened, and Mr. Harrison walked in. The tall, thin teacher was straight out of teacher training college and was a prime target for the taunts and misbehaviour from the students who always seemed to be able to sense fear in the new teachers.

"Okay, settle down everyone," Mr Harrison started. "I have some fun for you today."

"Is it true we're gonna chop up some frogs, sir?" a voice shouted from the back.

"Yes, Simon. Now this will be done in pairs, so make sure you are in your lab pairs and then one of each come up to collect your frogs."

"I'll go and get ours," Tracy said, putting her hand on Zachary's knee. "You rest up."

Zachary groaned inside as he realised that, by getting injured in the fight right before having class with Tracy, it would give her the next opportunity to try to get him to ask her out. He hadn't yet figured girls out, preferring to play on Bobby's computer, or the made-up games from their Dungeons and Dragons sets. He knew that girls had a fascination for him, but it was something that he was still to experience. To be honest, it scared him a little. What if he killed them, like he had his own mother.

He glanced across to where Freddie was sitting. The normally brash boy was slumped in his chair, seemingly trying to hide from all and sundry, as Philippa bounced back to their joint desk with the container holding a green unanimated object.

"Here we are," Tracy's excited voice said as she placed their container down on the desk in front of him.

Zachary glanced down and saw the very dead frog stretched out. He reached down and picked it up, turning it over and over in his hand.

"Okay class. Put on your surgical gloves, and we will start with an incision across the belly, from here to here." Mr Harrison pointed to a screen which showed the image of a frog.

"You do it, Zachary," Tracy said, suddenly looking rather green in her complexion.

Cries of yuk, gross and disgusting came from around the room, but Zachary seemed to be in a trance as he skilfully followed the directions from the teacher and dissected the frog, poking around and pulling out various body parts with fascination.

Tracy watched him with her own look of fascination. *He is going to become a doctor or something, that's why he's like this,* she thought. She glanced down and gagged at the now fully vivisected amphibian.

"Are you okay?" Zachary asked, hearing the girl's moan.

"I'm okay," she smiled back weakly. "I'm glad that you are my partner 'cos I don't think I could have done that."

"Done what?" Zachary asked before glancing

down. He frowned. "Oh, that … well I guess that I knew you wouldn't want to do it."

She gave him a smile which showed off her dimples. Zachary felt a small quiver in his stomach and returned a shy smile.

Tracy's heart gave a quick, excited beat of triumph as she realised that she had broken through the first of whatever barriers Zachary had been putting up. She rubbed his knee and cursed as the bell rang, signalling the end of class.

"I'll see you at lunch?" she asked.

"Erm … maybe," he replied. He picked up his bag and hurriedly left the room, wanting to find solace somewhere so that he could think about what was happening with Tracy.

Zachary managed to evade Tracy's attention at lunch by simply avoiding her altogether and not going into the canteen. He found a tree in the playground and sat underneath it, thoughts running through his head. A shadow fell over him.

"Hey squirt, what are you doing?"

Zachary looked up, fearing that he was about to be attacked.

"Kenny?" He breathed a sigh of relief. He saw Dicky and Jack standing behind his brother.

"What the fuck did you do to Freddie?"

"Freddie and his mates jumped me at break. I didn't mean to hurt them or anything."

"I didn't know you could fight," Kenny said, as the three older boys took a seat next to Zachary. "I haven't taught you, so where did you learn to fight like that?"

"I don't know," Zachary said. "One minute they were kicking me, and then I was stood over them."

"Freddie deserves it," Dicky said. "Peter's brother is a little shit. He thinks he's the big bollocks, so someone needed to take him down a peg or two."

"Still, it's Peter's brother," Jack said. "He's going to cause shit for this."

"You didn't do nothing when he's beaten me up before." A flat tone came out of Zachary's mouth. Kenny glanced at him and saw the same expression he had seen when his brother had hit his dad.

"Yeah, I know. I'm sorry about that. I was a jerk, okay?"

"Zachary can look after himself now."

The three older boys looked at him, confusion showing on their faces.

"Why are you talking about yourself in the third person?" Dicky asked.

"What does that mean?" Jack queried.

"Why am I doing what?" Zachary asked, his voice seemingly normal again.

112

"You called yourself Zachary," Kenny said. He stared at his brother, his eyes searching for a sign that there was something wrong. Guilt ran through him as he realised that if there was anything wrong with his brother, it could be his fault.

"No idea what you're talking about," the young boy shrugged.

The bell rang to end the lunch break and they all stood up to head into the final classes of the day.

"Look, Zack," Kenny started. "Be careful of Peter, 'cos if he thinks that you hurt Freddie on purpose, he'll come after you. I'll warn him off, but he's a bit crazy, you know."

"I know." Zachary paused before turning and hugging Kenny. Kenny blushed for a moment, not normally allowing any affection for his brother to be displayed in front of his friends, before returning the hug. He let go and punched Zachary lightly on the arm.

"Go study!"

The end of the school day arrived with the news that Bobby was being held in detention for throwing his dissected frog at Carly Winters, causing the blonde girl to vomit as the entrails slapped across her face.

Zachary shook his head at the news. *Typical Bobby!*

Heading out of the school gates, he felt the first droplets of rain on his face. He glanced up at the sky and saw dark grey clouds rolling towards the school.

"Shit, I forgot my coat," he muttered as he started to jog. He spied the alleyway that led to Spring Road, knowing that it was a good shortcut home. With no Bobby, he didn't need to go "the long way round" to walk past his friend's house so he cut through the alleyway.

The drizzle picked up intensity, turning into a steady downpour and Zachary had his head down, trying to stop the rain from getting into his eyes and down the front of his shirt, which as soon as school was finished, was unbuttoned at the top with the purple school tie loosened.

He didn't see the sudden appearance of the boys from the small bush on the right of the alleyway. The first that he knew he was in trouble was when his hands scraped along the gravel path, sharp shards of stone cutting into his hands, as he stopped himself from faceplanting into the path.

"Beat up my little brother will you, shit head," Peter Kenton snarled as he repeatedly kicked Zachary in his ribs.

Zachary whimpered in pain, and he had a moment of déjà vu from the fight earlier in the morning.

He felt pain in his back where Ian Hollis joined in

with his friend. The pair of older boys continued their onslaught as Zachary curled himself into a ball.

"Fuckwits! Leave him alone!" Kenny's voice echoed down the alleyway as he sprinted towards his two supposed friends who were beating up his brother. He'd left Jack and Dicky in his wake as he rushed to help his brother. Launching himself at Peter, he threw punch after punch, forcing the boy back from the prone body of Zachary.

Ian turned and flew backwards as Jack's fist connected with his jaw. "Stay down prick!" Jack snarled.

Dicky bent over Zachary's body and staggered backwards as his fist threw a punch in defence of what he assumed was another attack. "Stop it Zack, it's me, Dicky."

"Oh, sorry," the boy said.

"I told you to leave him alone, now fuck off before I kill you," Kenny hissed as he threw one final punch.

Ian grabbed the swaying Peter and the pair staggered away into the distance.

"Are you okay?" Kenny said, crouching down to his brother. "I warned you to watch out for them."

"I didn't see them."

"Why aren't you with Bobby?"

"He got detention."

"Then you should have waited for me."

"I can look after myself."

"Obviously!" The harsh sarcasm dripped from Kenny's voice before turning gentle. "Can you get up?"

"Uh-huh."

Dicky and Kenny helped the boy to his feet and, despite a few twinges of pain, Zachary declared himself fit enough to walk, although he did lean on his brother as they made their way home.

Having said their goodbyes to Dicky, Kenny helped Zachary up to his room and told him to rest up.

"But I've gotta do the bins or Dad'll go mad."

"I'll take care of it and will persuade Dad that I want a takeaway for dinner tonight, so you don't have to cook."

"Thanks, Kenny."

Three hours later, the door to Zachary's room burst open.

"Where is he?" The slurring voice of Harvey Downes shouted.

"Zack? Zack?" Kenny jumped in front of his dad,

wanting to protect his brother from the rage of his now drunken father.

"What?" Zachary's sleepy voice sounded from the bed. He sat up, grimacing at his wet clothes. "Oh shit, I'm sorry Dad. I didn't mean to wet again."

The boy flinched as Harvey strode across the room to slap the boy around the head. "Get that mess cleaned up."

He turned and left.

Zachary's eyes dribbled tears as he looked up at his brother, who he was expecting to turn away in disgust at him.

"Where were you?" Kenny asked quietly.

"What do you mean? I've been here since we got home from school."

"No, you weren't. You must have been sleepwalking again." Kenny came over to the bed and, with a hint of hesitation, bent down and sniffed the wet bedsheets. "That's not piss, that's just water. You got soaked sleepwalking."

Chapter 12

May 2021

The office was silent. DI Michaels stood at the front, not wanting to look at the pictures that were on the screen in front of him.

"Okay, people. This is a bad one," he said.

"That's what you said about Mary Hopkins, boss," Paula Smith muttered.

"This is worse."

"Why? Just because it's a male?"

"DS Smith, I know that you have your political agenda with the domestic abuse register, but this is not the time nor the place." Will Michaels frowned at her. "You want that register, then maybe this is another piece of the jigsaw. This isn't just 'a male', it's a teenage boy, thirteen or fourteen years of age."

"What?" Bobby Hemmings asked. "You're kidding. Who would do that to a kid?"

The photographs scrolling through on the screen showed shocking images of the remains of a young boy, his body parts scattered over a small area. Zack's stomach turned as he saw blood splatter after blood splatter on the green foliage.

"Isn't that Kipling Copse?" Zack asked. "That's the woods just off Ambra Vale East."

"You know your geography, DC Jacobs," The forensic officer, Darren Green said as he nodded. "Early this morning, a Mr Robert Waddle was walking his dog through the woods and came across the body. He rang 999 immediately and we were despatched to the scene. The remains have been transferred to the lab and the area has been sealed off from the public."

"Have we identified the body yet?" Bobby asked.

"Not yet. The teeth were smashed so dentals aren't giving us much, and we are looking at school records for a match to the face."

The room shuddered collectively as the picture of the boy's face flashed on screen. It was bruised beyond immediate recognition, but something tugged at the memory of Zack.

"Have you tried running prints?"

"Why? He's just a kid." Will Michaels said. "It will be hard anyway as the boy's fingers were mangled so badly that we don't know if we can get them straight enough to get a print."

"I sort of recognise him from the files in the Mary Hopkins case," Zack said. He left the meeting room, went to his desk and pulled out a large file. On his return, he flicked through the file until he found the picture he was looking for.

Holding it up alongside the picture of the victim, he turned to Will.

"Look, the same colour eyes, the nose, the hair. Obviously, the jaw can't be matched, but my gut says it's him."

"Who's that?" Will asked.

"Marc Woods. He is one of Dan Hopkins' friends. The gang of them seem to be a nasty bunch of kids, but come on, someone has butchered him."

"Isn't that the lad who broke Oliver Williams' fingers?" Bobby asked.

"What's this?" Will asked.

"A couple of months ago, there was an incident where an eleven year old budding pianist had his fingers broken by a gang. Marc was the main suspect but there wasn't enough evidence to prove anything, so CPS wouldn't prosecute. Yesterday, Bobby and I were called to the Royal Infirmary as Oliver had been attacked again, fingers broken, and a witness placed three of Dan's friends at the scene as the attackers. Marc was the main instigator.

Looks like someone was out for revenge."

"Darren, have you been able to get prints off the remains?" Will asked.

"We have but hadn't thought about running them as, well, it's just a kid for fuck's sake."

"Run them. If it is Marc, then his prints are on file from when he was picked up previously."

"Aren't we supposed to remove innocent prints?" Zack asked.

"Well, yes, but sometimes the paperwork is delayed going through," Will said with a shrug. He could see Paula bristle. "Again, now is not the time for the do-gooder complaints DS Smith. Do I make myself clear?"

She nodded, a sour expression on her face.

"This is the second murder in the space of two weeks. We will soon be getting pressure from above, and the press, about what is going on and we need answers, and we need them fast.

"We aren't the largest force, but I don't want to bring another force into this. Can we cope with looking into both?"

"Yes boss," came the collective reply.

"Okay then. Paula, you're with me and we will go and look at the scene. Zack, I want you and Bobby to take a run at Richard Hopkins, although from what I understand, you did that already Zack?"

"Ah, well, um …"

"Don't worry. I trust you, and there haven't been any repercussions. If we can't find anything linking him, other than his confession which to be honest, is so full of holes that CPS will dismiss it immediately, then we will have to release him tonight."

"Boss, there is one thing …" Bobby said. "Erm, I shouldn't mention it really but if the boy in the woods is Marc Wood, well, erm, Oliver Williams is Lawrence Williams' nephew."

"You think Lawrence could have something to do with it?" Will asked, surprised.

"He was pretty upset when he found out that Richard was Dan's father and Dan is mates with Marc. When he came to the Royal yesterday afternoon to pick up Oliver, he was saying all sorts of stupid things."

"I'm sure that he didn't mean them," Zack said. "It would have just been the anger and frustration talking."

"Still, it's something to keep in mind," Will sighed. "However unpleasant it may be."

The grey paint on the inside of the interview room seemed even more depressing than it had before. Bobby and Zack took the seats opposite Richard, who was alone.

Zack handed across a plastic cup filled with a murky brown liquid.

"Sorry, the machine stuff is pretty unpleasant," he apologised.

"Thanks," Richard said as he absently sipped it.

Bobby pressed the record buttons on the tape machine and there were three long beeps.

"Interview commencing with Richard Hopkins; dated 21st May 2021. Present are DC Zachary Jacobs, PC Robert Hemmings. Mr Hopkins has turned down legal counsel and continues to represent himself," Zack said into the tape.

"Richard, I'll be honest with you here and we need the same from you. Your confession has inconsistences within it, and we have also been able to place you at your workplace at the time when, according to our forensic team, the murder of Mary took place."

"But it wasn't Dan," Richard started.

"Richard, by continuing to lie about this, you are holding up our enquiries and could be charged with obstructing a police investigation. If we charge you with that, you would be removed as a suspect in Mary's death anyway."

Richard's face looked distraught. "Zack, sorry, DC Jacobs. You have to believe me. Dan didn't do this."

"I believe you, but we need you to withdraw your confession so that we can properly investigate and then clear Dan. Until we clear the pair of you, we cannot proceed with finding out who did actually murder Mary."

Richard looked his old school friend in the eye. He saw the honesty in it. "I trust you. Should I call for counsel or can it just be my word?"

"A written statement will do," Zack said. "I'll persuade the DI not to press charges about obstruction as I am sure that we can all understand your initial panic about wanting to protect your son."

"Thank you."

"I will send in a legal clerk to draft the statement with you and will let DI Michaels know. He will need to sign off on the release. You should be home by the morning at the latest."

"Will Dan be able to come home as well?"

"I'll have to check but, as you will no longer be a suspect, I don't see any reason why not."

"Can you let him know, and tell him I'm sorry for everything that's happened to him."

"Tell him tomorrow when you see him."

Zack pressed stop on the tapes and stood. He shook Richard's hand. "You always looked out for me when we were at school. It's my turn to return the favour."

They left the room, instructing the duty sergeant

to fetch a legal clerk and then to return Richard to his holding cell.

"Well, the boss is going to shit a brick," Bobby said. "But I think you're right. I've been thinking a lot about the past, and Dicky always did seem to be a nice guy."

They were about to walk into their office when Darren Green rushed up to them. "Your hunch was bang on, DC Jacobs."

"What do you mean?"

"The boy. It is Marc Wood, well, was Marc Wood."

"Shit."

"At least we have a starting place and a motive. I'm trying to get hold of DI Michaels, but Kipling Copse is notorious for being a black spot for any type of phone signal."

"Well, keep trying! He needs to know."

"We could go out there," Bobby started but saw Zack shake his head. "Ah no, I just remembered. We've got that report to file."

They watched Darren turn and walk back down to his department before Bobby turned to Zack.

"So, we aren't going to the scene because?"

"Because I want another run at Dan, before he

goes home, and before the news about Marc is made public."

"You think he has had something to do with this?"

"No, of course not. He's in protective custody at the moment so wouldn't have had a chance, but I want more background on this little bullying gang of theirs. While I don't think he's guilty of Mary's murder, there is more to it than meets the eye here."

Bobby pulled into the driveway of the semi-detached house that the department used as a safe house for witnesses or other persons of interest. Zack knocked on the door and they showed their IDs before walking through into the lounge.

Dan was slouched on the sofa wearing a t-shirt, boxer shorts and white trainer socks. He held a PS4 controller in his hands and was squirming and fidgeting as the soldier that he was controlling ran through whichever battlefield the latest Call of Duty game was set in.

"Dan, can we have a word please?" Zack started.

"In a minute," the boy said. "I'm about through this section."

"We need to talk," Bobby said, his tone harsh.

"It's fine, Bobby. I know what it's like when you are nearly through a zone," Zack said. "We'll grab a cuppa from the kitchen while you finish up."

They left the boy and walked through to the kitchen where a plain clothed policewoman was cooking.

"Hi Kerri, how's things?" Zack greeted her.

"Oh Zack, it's you. This is a bit boring, but hey, I'll take an easy assignment any day."

"How's he been?"

"The kid? Very mixed actually. There are times when he is a little angel, wanting to please whoever is on duty, but then there are times when he is a right swine, shouting and acting up."

"You've got to remember that he's a fourteen year old kid who's just lost his stepmother and his father is being held for it."

"I know, which is why we tread lightly when he tantrums. He's quite a strong lad. Eric is sporting a fantastic shiner from two days ago when things got heated."

"He deserved it," Dan's voice came from behind them. "He said that my dad was a murderer."

Zack looked over at Kerri who shrugged. "I wasn't on duty," she said. "But you know how abrasive Eric can be at times. He shouldn't really have been assigned to Dan." She smiled at the boy, whose face lit up.

"Okay, well Dan, if you've finished the zone and

saved it, we need to have a chat," Zack said.

"Shit! I forgot to save!"

The boy dashed back into the lounge and, as they followed him in, saw him flop down onto the sofa, a look of relief on his face.

"It's taken me four days to get to this level, and all day to kill the powered-up guy. That would have been bad if I didn't save!"

"I know what you mean," Bobby sniggered. They all looked at him. "What can I say, I'm a gamer. I nearly got all the way through the Last of Us 2 when we had that power cut a month ago. I lost nine hours of work."

"Ah, I'd love to try that game. The first one was amazing!"

"Looks like we've got a couple of gamer buddies here!" Zack sighed.

"Oh, come off it," Bobby hit back. "Remember the good old days of Zelda and Final Fantasy."

"You guys are cool," Dan said. He hung his head. "Sorry for being a jackass before."

Zack reached out and patted his arm. "That's okay. Now we have some good news. Your dad has retracted his statement about killing your mum."

"Stepmother," Dan growled.

"So, once all of the legals go through, he will be released without charge, and you will be able to go home to him."

"That's awesome," Dan bubbled. "I told you he didn't do it."

"And you were right." Zack said.

"We will still need to ask you some more questions about what happened, so that we can clear you as well," Zack started. "But we can't do that without Mr Gillespie being present."

"I like him," Dan said. "I thought he was a perv at first, but he's been looking out for me."

"He does that," Bobby said. "He can be a pain in the butt for us, but he does protect his clients."

"So why are you here? What did you want to talk about?" Dan asked, a look of trepidation and confusion on his face.

"Okay, Dan, now this isn't anything that you are going to get into trouble about," Zack started.

Dan immediately stiffened and Zack placed a hand on his knee to reassure him.

"We just need to ask you some questions about your friends."

"Why?"

Bobby glanced at Zack who nodded.

"Oliver Williams was attacked yesterday on the way home from school."

"Is he okay?"

"No, he had his fingers broken again."

"Fucking Marc," Dan cussed. "I told him to leave him be, that he'd got the message last time."

"What message?" Zack asked.

"Oli likes Marc's sister, but Marc won't let her date anyone."

"So, you knew that it was Marc who attacked him last time?" Zack asked gently.

"Yeah, Libby was bragging about how they beat up the golden boy of the school."

"You weren't involved?"

"Nah, I didn't have anything against the kid. I thought he was alright," Dan said. "I sort of like classical music, and Oli was really good, like really really good on the piano." He paused. "Don't tell anyone I like that sort of music, it would ruin my cred, you know."

"I know," Bobby chuckled.

"What about Tony?"

"Gwynnis?"

"Huh?"

"Sorry, that's what we call him to wind him up. His surname is Gwynne, so Gwynnis, like in Glennis. It's kind of lame. Philip came up with it."

"Was he involved the first time?"

"Don't think so, he is sort of fixated on Philip,"

Dan said. "Look, with everything that's gone on, and talking with Kerri, I know that I've sort of been a bad kid. I've been a bully, especially with my cousin. We all have been. Kerri's real nice and I told her about, you know, what Mary was making me do, and we think it was a way of me hitting out without it being at Mary, 'cos she scared me. So, I picked on younger kids to show that I was strong."

A tear trickled down Dan's cheek. "I need to say that I'm sorry to Philip, and Kerri reckons that there are people who can help me with my anger and get over what she did to me."

Bobby reached around and placed a comforting hand on Dan's shoulder and, for once, he did not reject the gesture.

"We'll make sure of it."

They left Dan in Kerri's capable hands and walked back to the car.

"That little bugger has grown on me," Bobby said. "We need to find out who killed Mary so we can clear his name as well."

Chapter 13

June 2000

Zachary woke the following morning to a clean and dry bed, but a throbbing pain in his head. He pulled back the covers and walked through to the bathroom. Deciding against a shower, he ran the water into the sink basin before looking up into the mirror.

A dark purple bruise bordered his left eye where his father had slapped him the night before. He touched it gently, wincing with the pain that shot through his brain.

He thought back to the dream that he'd had during the night. It was a weird combination of horror and pleasure, of standing up to his father, of escaping the hell hole of his home and finding a loving parent.

His thoughts immediately went to Mr Jacobs, his English and form teacher. He had always looked out for him, and he found himself wishing that he was Mr Jacobs' son, not the son of a drunken bum of a father.

"Come on Zack, I need a piss," Kenny shouted through the door.

"Well, come and have one then," he snapped back.

"With you in there?"

"Scared I'm bigger than you?" Zachary laughed. For a moment, he didn't recognise the tone of his voice, but for some reason, he felt brave and strong.

The door opened and his older brother walked in. He scowled at Zachary who shrugged, got undressed and had a quick stand-up wash.

"You should shower," Kenny said.

"I didn't pee, so I don't need to," Zachary replied.

He heard the stream from Kenny hitting the toilet bowl and ignored him. Drying himself with a towel, he left the bathroom, the door wide open.

"Close the door, you perv!" Kenny shouted.

As the pair sat across from each other at the kitchen table, Kenny eyed his younger brother.

"Where were you last night?"

"Sleepwalking like you said. I must have gone round the garden or something, 'cos my shoes were covered in mud. I've cleaned them, so don't worry, Dad's not gonna slap me again."

"You need to stop that," Kenny said. "For a start off, there's the curfew. The police will do their nut, and then so will Dad. You need to act cool around him. Something isn't right with him just now. He's a lot angrier than normal."

"Tell me about it," Zachary said, pointing to his eye. "How come he never hits you?"

Kenny bit his lip. He didn't want to say the words that could damage his younger brother. It was weird how everything seemed to have changed since the deaths had started. Kenny had grown up hating his brother for killing his mother, something which he knew was irrational, but he was the easy target for his anger over losing her.

Since the murders, he was worried about how his friends were being targeted, almost as though the murderer was building up to something big. He looked at the bruised face of his younger brother. He looked so much like the photos of his mother that Kenny had vowed to protect him from whoever it was that was killing his friends.

He had that gnawing, horrible, pit of the stomach feeling that, somehow, his dad was involved. His dad hated Zachary. He took every opportunity to belittle him, to slap him around. In the past, Kenny revelled in his brother's misery and pain but now, he only wanted it to stop. He had already vowed to kill anyone who seriously hurt Zachary, and that included his own father.

"Come on, eat up. We need to get to school. You're walking with me just in case those idiots try to jump you again."

"But I walk with Bobby," Zachary complained.

"Then we will pick him up on the way."

The walk to school was largely uneventful. Bobby was surprised to see Kenny with Zachary but, as they turned the corner of the street that led to the school gates, they saw several police cars parked in the school parking bays.

Scores of parents were milling around, and Zachary saw DS Michaels talking to a representative group of them. Mr Saddler, the headmaster, was talking with another group, while several teachers, including Mr Jacobs, were ushering the students inside.

"What's going on, Mr Jacobs?" Kenny asked as they approached the school door.

"There's an assembly for everyone," Sammy replied before glancing at Zachary. "What the hell?" He reached out and turned the boy's face towards him. "Did your dad do this?"

Zachary could hear the underlying anger in his teacher's voice but instead of frightening him, it soothed him. He realised that Mr Jacobs cared about him, and his thoughts flashed back to the dream that he'd had.

"He fell over, sleepwalking, last night, sir," Kenny said quickly. He took his brother's elbow and half led; half dragged him inside.

"Why didn't you let me answer," Zachary hissed, his voice dropping to a low tone.

"You know why," Kenny snapped back. "If they report Dad, then the police will arrest him, and we'll end up in care."

"Maybe that's a good thing."

"Erm, what are you guys talking about?" Bobby asked, standing to one side. He was afraid of Kenny, and his gang, and he really didn't want to upset the older boy, but he had to stick up for his friend.

"Nothing. You forget this conversation happened or I'll come for you," Kenny snarled, raising a clenched fist at the young boy.

Bobby nodded and quickly walked down the corridor towards the main hall where the assembly was being held.

"Come on," Kenny said, taking hold of Zachary and marching him along to the hall. They took seats near the back, and were joined by Jack, Ian and Dicky.

"What do you think is going on?" Dicky asked.

"Dunno, but it's nothing good. I saw DS Michaels outside. He was the one who I saw talking with Jason's parents," Kenny said.

"You think there's been another murder?" Ian asked.

"How do I know?" Kenny shrugged. "Where's Peter?"

They looked around but couldn't see their friend. Zachary spotted Philippa Higgins who, for once, was sitting next to Tracy and not next to Freddie. He stood up and scoured the assembled students before sitting back down.

"Freddie isn't here either," he said softly to the others.

"Maybe they've got a bug?" Dicky suggested hopefully.

"Well, we are about to find out," Kenny said, and nudged the others. They looked up and saw DS Michaels and Mr Saddler walk onto the stage in front of the school.

Zachary noticed that a lot of the parents from outside had also been invited into the school, with a lot of the younger students sitting next to their respective parents.

Mr Saddler walked to the front of the stage, and Zachary noticed that he had a microphone in his hand, instead of relying on his natural booming voice.

"Settle down everyone, please," he started. "We have some difficult news for you. A few people know him, but I would like to introduce Detective Sergeant William Michaels from Bristol Police to address you all. Please do not interrupt him and we will take any questions at the end."

He turned and handed the microphone to DS Michaels, who paused for a moment looking out across the assembled students. His eyes seemed to fall on Kenny, Ian, Jack and Zachary before moving back to the front.

"As you are aware, we have experienced the deaths of two of your fellow students, Jason Billings and George Adams. It is with great sadness that we have to report that Peter Kenton has also fallen victim to this unknown killer."

Cries and screams echoed around the hall.

"Please. Let me continue. Your fellow student, Freddie Kenton is at home with his family, and we are offering full support to them, along with the Billings and Adams families. At this time, we are still investigating leads, but this does look like it is the work of a single person."

"A serial killer?" someone shouted from the right of Zachary.

"Whilst we are not ruling anything out, there are similarities to the murders that would suggest it is the work of a single person. Please be assured that the full weight of the Bristol Police Force is now behind us, leaving no stone unturned, until we catch the perpetrator.

"However, until the person is apprehended, it has been agreed with the Mayor, the MP, the Police Commissioner and the School Governing Bodies that, with immediate effect, a full curfew will now be imposed on all children under the age of sixteen. You will be allowed to leave your homes only during school hours. You are to arrive on time and go straight home. Any child found to be outside their home after this time will be picked up by one of our patrols and returned home with a warning. A second offence will result in a fine for the parents and a third offence will involve taking the child into care."

The hall erupted with cries of 'what!', 'you can't lock us up!' and other shouts of anger and frustration.

"I know that this is harsh, but it is the best way we can keep you safe and help us find this person as quickly as possible."

Mr Saddler took the microphone back from DS Michaels.

"Okay, I am sure that some parents may have further questions so, students, please can you head to your form rooms for registration, we can answer any questions from your parents. Thank you."

The bell rang and the students stood, as one, scrambling to the exits and the loud noise of frightened and angry chatter followed them en masse through the corridors leading to the form rooms.

Kenny held on to Zachary's arm for a moment as the swarm of students threatened to carry them along the corridor.

"Look Zack, be careful, okay." Kenny stared at the bruise on his brother's face. "Meet me by the front gate when school finishes and we'll walk home together. Bring Bobby as well, if you want."

"Okay," Zachary replied, seeing kindness in Kenny's eyes.

"I love you, bro," Kenny said, ruffling Zachary's hair before turning and heading off towards his form room.

Of course, the teachers struggled to get any attention to classwork from the students that day, and so resigned themselves to holding discussions about what was happening and what it meant.

Zachary and Bobby sat quietly next to each other, Bobby eyeing his friend with a wary look.

"What?" Zachary said, a little harsher than he meant.

"Did your dad hit you?" Bobby whispered.

"I fell."

"Bullshit. I've seen the bruises in the past, Zack. I

thought it was Kenny and his mates, but if it's your dad, you've got to tell someone."

"Kenny says they'll put us in care if I do."

"Got to be better than being slapped around?"

"I've heard about kids who go into care. Stuff happens to them."

Bobby looked at the fear in his friend's eyes and decided for the moment to drop the subject. "So, Peter is dead. That's three of Kenny's mates. Who do you think has it in for them?"

"I dunno, but in a way, is it wrong to say that I don't care that they're dead?" Zachary's eyes started to well up. He wiped the tears away before anyone else saw them.

"What do you mean?"

"They were mean and nasty to me, they hit me a lot. You were right in that most of my bruises were from Kenny and them, but ever since the murders, Kenny's completely changed. It's like he's gone full circle from hating me to protecting me."

"You don't think it could be Kenny, do you?"

"Kenny? Doing what?"

"The murders?"

"Don't be stupid. They're his friends."

"But they were hurting you and now they're dead. It's something to think about."

"Something else to worry about, you mean?"

The bell finally rang to end a very traumatic day for the school students. As Zachary and Bobby slowly walked through the doors that lead to one of the many playgrounds, Zachary's thoughts drifted to Bobby's suggestion.

Could Kenny be the murderer? He had certainly changed since they jumped him in the woods and Kenny found out that Jason had been abusing Nate. Poor Nate. I must see how he is.

The pavement raced up as Zachary was tripped from behind.

"Leave him alone," Bobby yelled as Ian and Jack jumped the pair. Jack was holding Bobby down, not a difficult task given the weight and size difference between the two.

Ian sat astride Zachary's chest. "Did your daddy beat you last night? What for? Being out past curfew?"

He slapped the boy.

"Get off me."

"This all started after that day in the woods. You're fucking cursed, you know that." Another two slaps rang out.

"Leave me alone." Zachary's voice dropped to a low tone and Ian paused for a moment, seeing a steely glare staring back from the boy underneath him. He shook it off.

"You're the fucking killer, aren't you?" Ian spat at the boy.

"Don't be stupid, Ian," Jack said. "How could he have killed the others?"

"Shut up and help me."

"I agreed to rough him up, not to go any further," Jack said, shaking his head, wondering if he had done the right thing in joining in with his friend.

Ian put his hand inside his school blazer and a flash of metal glinted in the summer sun. There was the sound of a click, a swish of a blade and Ian held aloft the small switchblade that he had had from his days as a cub scout.

"Ian, what the fuck?" Dicky Hopkins' voice rang out from a few yards away. "Get the fuck off him."

"He's the fucking killer and, if I kill him, he won't be able to kill again."

"You're nuts," Dicky said and launched himself at his friend. He knocked Ian off the young boy, and there was a clattering sound of the knife as it skittered across the playground.

"He killed Peter, I know it," Ian sobbed. "He killed Peter."

Dicky grabbed hold of Ian and the boy broke down. He motioned to Jack to get the two younger boys away.

"What the fuck was that about?" Bobby

demanded as they rounded the corner and saw Kenny waiting impatiently.

"Don't tell your brother this happened," Jack said quietly.

"Why did you attack us? Why is Ian so cut up about Peter and not the others?" Zachary asked.

"I guess they'd hidden it well," Jack said. "Only a few of us knew. Peter and Ian were boyfriends."

Chapter 14

May 2021

DI Will Michaels sighed as he looked across his desk. His adopted nephew Zack was flicking through photographs, a frown on his face.

"Zack, I'm not sure it's a good idea that you get involved with the Marc Wood case as well as Mary Hopkins."

"Why Uncle Will?" Zack asked, not raising his gaze. He was focused upon the grisly scenes that the pictures laid out in front of him. "You didn't want me on the Mary Hopkins case in the first place."

"I didn't want you near the Mary Hopkins case because of your connection to Richard ..."

"But that has worked out for the best," Zack replied. "Richard isn't the killer, and now we are in the process of clearing him, we can work on clearing Dan, who is a victim here as well. Then we can go and find the real killer."

"Admittedly, your gut feeling has borne out with Richard. I want you to concentrate on that case and leave the Marc Wood case to Paula."

"Boss, with all due respect to Paula, she's blinded with her political agenda. I think she would be better with the Hopkins case, but anyway …" Zack paused. "I think the two are connected."

"What? Why?" Will let an exasperated sigh escape his control. "Don't tell me, your gut."

"All I am saying is that someone murdered Mary Hopkins, the stepmother of Daniel. She was abusing the lad. Now someone has killed Marc, a friend of Dan's who was also a known bully and someone who had twice assaulted Oliver Williams." Zack took a breath. "There has to be a connection, I just can't piece it together yet."

Will looked at the intense frown on Zack's face and knew that he was right. "Okay, I will let you both to see if there is a link. For now, I want you to drop past legals and get Richard's sign off papers and get him home. Then we can try to figure this all out, but we need to do it fast. I am already getting grief."

"Will do, boss," Zack smiled and stood to leave. "Thanks for not benching me on this one. I know that you think I'll have issues with what happened with my father, but trust me, I'm fine. Dad did a good job getting me through it."

"Have you been to see him?"

Zack felt a twinge of guilt. "I will. Soon, I promise."

"I know it's hard for you, but just remember, he is still the man who raised you, who helped you. You can remember him even if he can't remember you."

"I'll go after I sort Richard out."

Zack walked into the holding area. He saw the burly Lawrence Williams behind the duty desk.

"How's Oliver?"

"He's back on medication," Lawrence growled. "He doesn't understand why that swine is constantly beating him up."

"I've been told it's something to do with Marc's sister, Lucy. Oliver apparently likes her, but Marc is overprotective." Zack saw Lawrence's face darken. "Look, I'm not condoning what he's done, far from it, just giving an insight. Besides, you don't need to worry about Marc hurting Oliver again."

"Why? Has someone done us all a favour and killed him?"

There was a silence.

"Shit. That boy in the woods. That's Marc?"

Lawrence seemed genuinely shocked.

"It's not officially released yet, but forensics matched the prints late yesterday."

A conflict of emotions ran across Lawrence's face, before settling on an unhappy one.

"That's bad. I mean, I know what I said, but honestly, I wouldn't have wanted the boy dead, really."

"Are you sure?"

"Are you shitting me, Zack? I'm a policeman. My duty is to protect the public, even the criminals, with the position I hold. I'm here to make sure no one hurts them while due process takes its course, and the law is upheld. Vigilantism is not acceptable in any form and for any reason."

"I know, Lawrence," Zack sighed. "I just wanted to catch you unawares, just in case."

"Well, you can strike me off your list of suspects, Detective."

Zack heard the frostiness in the tone and realised that it would take some time for this bridge to be rebuilt. He handed across the release papers for Richard and stood silently as Lawrence left him at the desk and went to retrieve him from his cell.

A smiling Richard greeted Zack and shook his hand.

"Sorry it took so long to get the paperwork

through," Zack said. "Legal had gone home by the time we processed it from this end, so we had to wait for them to get in this morning."

"It's fine," Richard said. "I'm just looking forward to seeing Dan."

Lawrence ran through Richard's belongings that had been taken from him on his arrest, and the pair left.

"Come on, I'll give you a lift," Zack said. "Do you want to go home, or do you want to stay at the house where we have Dan?"

"Is Dan allowed to come back with me?"

"Of course," Zack replied. "Whilst we still have him as a person of interest, we are sure that he isn't the murderer. I managed to get him into protective custody so that he didn't end up in a care home. That certainly would have done nobody any favours, least of all Dan."

"You're a good friend, Zachary," Richard said.

"God, I haven't gone by Zachary since I was a kid."

"Well, you were always a good kid. I'm just sorry that I didn't do more to help you."

"You did enough."

The silence that followed was one full of emotion as each of them thought back to their youth, and the incidents around the demise of their friends.

Zack coughed and turned on the radio and pulled out of the car park.

"DAD!" Dan shouted exuberantly as he ran out of the front door and leapt into Richard's arms.

"I'm so sorry, Dan," Richard hugged the boy, tears streaming down his face. "I just wanted to protect you this time, after failing to stop her."

"It's not your fault, Dad," Dan cried. "She threatened that she'd kill you if I didn't do what she wanted. She was sick."

"It's all over now, son."

"Is it? Can we go home?" Dan looked at Zack.

"It's almost over, but yes, you can go home now."

"Can Kerri come with us?"

"Who's Kerri?" Richard asked.

"Kerri is ace. Come on, you've got to meet her." Dan grabbed Richard's hand and dragged him into the house, Zack following a few paces behind.

After the introductions were made, it took a couple of hours to load up Dan's belongings into the car and Zack drove them home. As they pulled into the driveway, Zack could see the nerves evident on the faces of the pair.

"There is going to be talk around your neighbours obviously, especially as the press got hold of the fact you had admitted it, Richard, but stick to your guns. Explain that you were doing it to protect Dan from any indication that it may have been him."

"They are gonna want to know why, though," Dan said in a small voice. "I'm gonna have to admit what she was doing."

"It's completely your choice," Zack said. "But to be honest, as bad as it sounds, it will probably help your cause with them. If your neighbours find out that she was abusing you, that you are the real victim here, then you will get their sympathy. It will help them understand your dad's actions as well, as he was just trying to protect you."

"We already have an audience," Richard said. "The curtain twitchers are out in full force."

Zack looked around and indeed, there were several curtains being pulled back slightly to allow the neighbours a view of the scene. He let out a disgusted sigh. "People should have better things to do than judge other people."

"Come on kiddo, let's go and face the music."

Zack put a hand on Richard's arm. "One last thing. We will have to release a statement saying that we have now released you without charge and you are no longer a suspect. The press are going to pick up on it, so expect them to be around. Don't lose your temper with them as they are still looking to pin Mary's murder on anyone. We are getting grief to solve this, especially with Marc's death as well."

"Marc's dead?" Dan's shocked gasp came from the back seat.

"Shit." Zack realised he had let it slip. "I'm sorry, Dan. I know he was your friend. It's not general knowledge yet, so please keep this quiet."

"But he's dead? How?"

"His body was found in Kipling Copse last night."

"That sounds like he was killed, not just died," Dan accused him.

"Yes, I am afraid it is. We think that someone killed Marc in retaliation for the attack on Oliver Williams."

"Marc was a nutter, but still, he was my mate. Who do you think did it?"

"Dan … leave the Detective alone for now. I am sure that they are looking into it," Richard said.

"I am on the case," Zack confirmed. "If we find anything out and, if I am allowed to, I will let you know."

They got out of the car and Zack helped them move Dan's belongings back into the family home. Saying a brief farewell, Zack decided that he needed some air and some time to process everything that was happening. He reached into the glove box and pulled out the file that contained the forensic notes regarding Marc Wood's death and he decided that he would go for a drive and get some time alone to think.

Libby Forrest slapped Henry Lavery's hand as it slipped inside the front of her blouse.

"Stop it!" she snapped as Henry nuzzled her neck.

"Come on, Libby," Henry moaned. "You promised me some action on my birthday."

"But not here, not in the woods."

"Why not," Henry complained, feeling his ardour rising. "There's no one around."

"What if someone catches us?"

"Then they get a show that they aren't allowed to admit to seeing," he sniggered. "We are underage, after all."

He kissed her deeply and Libby's willpower went. She did love Henry and knew that she wanted him to be her first. She just wasn't sure if she should wait until they were older.

"Okay, listen. We're not going all the way, but we can strip off a bit."

Henry grinned and pulled off his shirt. He faced his girlfriend of six years and undid the buttons on her blouse. Seeing her breasts for the first time pushed him over the edge. He pulled her closer to him, kissing her deeply once again before rolling backwards and pulling her on top of him.

His hands caressed her back and edged downwards to her short skirt. Pushing his luck, he started edging the skirt hem up.

Libby felt a slight panic at Henry's attempts to undress her fully and she started to squirm.

"Let me do it," Henry said, a hint of force in his voice.

There was a snap of a twig. The pair of lovers froze and, as one, looked in the direction of the interruption.

"Ah, sorry guys," Philip Whitehall said, his face flushing as red as the Bristol City football shirt that he was wearing. "I, er, was just out walking."

"You were watching us, you little pervert," Libby spat and rolled off Henry.

Philip stared at the half naked girl, unable to move.

"Told you he was a pervert," Libby said as she walked towards the transfixed boy. "Bet you want to touch them, don't you?"

"Ah, er, no," the boy's voice trembled but his eyes were firmly fixed on the first naked breasts that he had ever seen.

"Go on, touch them."

Philip's hand moved of its own accord, his brain screaming at it to stop. Just as it was about to touch the naked flesh, Libby slapped it away.

"Like I would let a little perv like you touch me," she spat. She slapped his face, which shocked Philip back into consciousness.

"I'm sorry," he stammered out, starting to turn away. "I'm gonna go."

"Oh no you're not," Henry snarled. "You think you can come here, spy on us, getting your perverted kicks and then try to touch my girl? Look, you've even got a boner," he said in disgust. "I'll make that go away."

He grabbed the boy's shoulders and brought his knee up, ramming it into Philip's groin.

Philip felt pain like never before and his high-pitched squeal set a nearby flock of birds scattering into the wind.

"Don't ever look at my girl again."

Kick after kick followed while, a now fully dressed, Libby took her favourite position, sitting on top of the boy to enable her to slap his face.

The sound of a car engine starting interrupted the pair of bullies for a moment. Seeing that the occupant was leaving the area, rather than coming to stop them, gave them renewed vigour and they returned their attention to the crying boy.

Chapter 15

June 2000

DS Michaels looked down at the sight in front of him. His heart sank. Blood was splattered everywhere. Worse than blood, body limbs were strewn across a small area of the woods.

He pitied the forensic team whose job it was to handle the mutilated corpse of the young boy. He walked over to DC Xavier Hollis.

"Have we identified the body yet?"

"Not yet," the grizzled veteran said. He ran his hand through his grey beard. "Forensics are still looking for the head." He sighed. "This isn't good. We've got a serial killer chopping up boys. What sick fuck does that?"

"An insane one," Will replied. "That's the only sane reason I could come up with. Why else would someone target boys like this?"

"I've only just been put onto the case, so I'm still catching up. Has there been any sign of sexual assault on them?"

"Why?"

"That could be another reason for mutilating the bodies, to distract or destroy evidence."

"Nice theory, but other than Jason Billings, there is no sign of any sexual activity with the other boys, and the only thing with Jason was the, ah, that his penis had been cut off and put in his mouth."

"Didn't you say that the boy had been abusing his brother?"

"Yes. I've interviewed Nate and it's not pretty stuff. The boy is in therapy now, helping him through. Jason had been abusing him for a number of years."

"He was the first victim? So that seems like a revenge killing."

"Nate was at home all evening."

"But if someone else knew, then they could have taken it into their own hands to stop him."

"You're making it sound like a vigilante killing," Will frowned. "Okay, I can go with that, but it doesn't explain the other boys."

"When we get back to the station, I'll have a look into who each boy was friends with, start drawing up comparisons. If each boy has wronged someone, there could be a common link."

"You know what, Xavier," Will said, clapping him on the shoulder. "That's the best idea that anyone has come up with. We're all chasing our tails on this and getting nowhere."

A shout from behind a tree interrupted them.

"I've found the head," a woman's voice shouted. "It's not pretty."

The pair of detectives walked around, and Will blanched at the sight. The young boy's face was twisted into a grimace of pain, the brown hair matted with blood. A silver knife was stuck inside the mouth.

Xavier gasped and dropped to his knees.

"What's wrong?" Will asked.

"That's Ian. That's my grandson."

The school was buzzing with the news of the latest murder. Grief counsellors had been brought in, as yet another student had been killed.

Sammy Jacobs stared at his English class as they chatted quietly and nervously. He had given up any hope of educating them today and, to be honest, he had no desire to inflict the misery of Shakespeare onto an already disturbed group of students.

He looked around, seeing who was silent, if there

were any of the students not coping with the news of Ian Hollis' murder. His eyes were drawn to Zachary Downes. He felt for the lad. Each of the victims had been friends of Zachary, or at least Zachary's brother, Kenny.

Sammy wondered how Jessica Brown was coping with Kenny in her class. Sammy didn't really know Zachary's older brother, just that he was a brash lad, but one that seemed to be able to take anything thrown his way. He hoped that Jessica was able to console him.

"Okay class, settle down for a moment," Sammy said. "I know that today is another shock. It's hurting us all. But we do need to try to concentrate on other things."

"How can we, sir?" Phillipa Higgins asked. "Someone is going around killing kids from our school! Who knows who will be next?"

"I am sure that the police are going to catch this person very soon," Sammy tried to reassure her.

"Either that or they will run out of students," Tracy muttered. She glanced across at Zachary who had his head down, his hands turning his pen over and over.

"Be that as it may, please can you pick up your books; we will go with something lighter today. Let's have a go at 'The Wind in the Willows'."

"That's a kid's book, sir," Colin Fenton whined.

"I hate to break it to you, Colin, but you're still kids," Sammy joked. "Okay then, as you think it's an easy read, why don't you start off."

Colin grimaced remembering that Mr Jacobs always picked on anyone who dissed the book choice. He opened the book to chapter one and started. "The Mole had been working very hard all the morning, spring-cleaning his little home,"

Sammy knew the book by heart. It had been one of his favourites as a child, his father reading it with him every evening from the age of six. He studied the class, most of the students were following along with Colin's words, knowing that at any time, he would stop whoever was reading and pick on someone else to take their turn.

A couple of boys at the back, the usual troublemakers, were passing notes to each other. Sammy had long given up on them, knowing that they had no interest in English Literature and would fail their GCSE without a care in the world.

Once again, his eyes fell on Zachary. The boy had the book open, his lips moving with the slow reading Colin, and absently turned each page on cue, but somehow, Sammy knew that Zachary's mind was elsewhere.

"Thank you, Colin. Zachary, will you take over please," Sammy said, wanting to get the boy's focus back to the book.

"Yes sir," Zachary said, although Sammy heard

the flat tone that the boy had used a few days ago before the fight with Freddie Kenton.

Sammy could only stand a couple of minutes listening to the monotoned dictation of the story before he asked Tracy Smith to take over. He knew that she loved reading, especially to her younger brother, and she always tried to put voices and inflections into her readings.

The bell rang to end the lesson and, as the students stood to gather their books into the bags, Zachary had remained seated.

"Aren't you coming Zack?" Tracy asked, taking the boy by the arm.

"Huh? What?" Zachary turned to look at her and, for a moment, Tracy thought she was looking at a different boy. She shook it off as he smiled at her. "Sorry, I must have zoned out."

"Zachary, can you stay behind for a moment," Sammy asked.

"I'll see you in biology," Tracy said.

"What is it, sir?" Zachary asked. "Mr Harrison doesn't like us being late to his class."

"I'll write you a note," Sammy said, taking a seat at the desk next to him. He thought he would try a different angle than the last time, no desk or chair to create a barrier between them.

Where to start? Sammy sighed.

"I know what you're going to ask, sir," Zachary said. "But honestly, I'm fine."

"Zachary, you're not. You are zoning out in class. You are distracted and not focusing. Other teachers are telling me the same, and I'm worried about you."

"Well, as long as I'm not a fourteen year old bully, I should be fine," Zachary said. Sammy immediately picked up the flat tone and knew that he was on dodgy ground with the boy.

"What do you mean by that?"

"Haven't you figured it out? Jason, George, Peter, Ian. They were all in Year 9. If it was random killings, surely there would be other ages?"

Sammy rocked back on his seat. "That is a very good insight," he said, making a mental note to ring his brother-in-law. He heard the classroom door open and the chatter of his Year 10 class starting to arrive.

"Off you go, you don't want to get in trouble with Mr Harrison."

"The note, sir?"

"What?

"You were going to give me a note."

Sammy quickly scribbled on a piece of paper and gave it to the boy, who left the room. As the Year 10 students took their seats, Sammy told them to start reading their required reading, 'The Catcher in the Rye' and excused himself to make his phone call to Will Michaels.

The school day passed quicky for some, and slowly for others. For Kenny Downes, it dragged along with the enthusiasm of a snail. His mind was in turmoil with the death of yet another of his gang. He was convinced someone was toying with him.

For Zachary, it passed quickly. He thought at one point that he had learned the art of teleportation, maybe like Nightcrawler from the X-Men comics that he loved, as he found himself leaving a classroom and then suddenly being in his next classroom, with no recollection of the journey in between.

Bobby was growing concerned, but Zachary brushed it off. At the end of the school day the two boys met Kenny at the school gates, which was now their routine. Bobby had grown to like Zachary's older brother in the last few days, having previously been on the wrong end of a few of Kenny's tantrums. Kenny had taken it on himself to walk his brother home and, as an adjunct, Bobby as well. With the murders that were happening, Bobby appreciated the gesture.

As they reached Bobby's home, he turned to say goodbye but could see Zachary had zoned out again. Not wanting to say anything, he muttered a goodbye and went inside.

The two brothers continued their walk home, Kenny silent in thought about his friends, while Zachary plodded along beside him. Reaching their home, they saw that their dad's car was parked in the driveway.

"Shit, that's not good," Kenny said. "He should still be at work."

Zachary had come out of his stupor and looked fearfully at his brother. "He could be drunk already."

"You go around the back into the garden, and I'll go inside," Kenny suggested. "I'll check out his mood and give you a call."

"It's my turn to cook. What if I mess up again?" Zachary absently rubbed his right arm where his dad had hit him the previous evening for dropping and smashing a plate as he cleared the dinner table.

"I'll help you, don't worry," Kenny said.

"I love you," Zachary said, giving his brother a brief hug, before silently creeping down the side passage of the house and into the back garden.

Kenny watched his brother until he had opened the back gate, took a breath, and went inside the front door.

The back garden was a mess. Despite the boys'

best efforts to keep on top of it, it was simply too large for the pair to manage without their dad's help. And Harvey Downes was no help to anyone. While his wife was alive, Harvey had managed to keep his drinking and his anger under control, but once she had died during Zachary's birth, he had been on a downward spiral ever since.

Zachary heard the shouting even before he had managed to close the back gate, and he knew that he would be in for a rough evening. He felt a splatter on his face, followed by another, then several. Looking up at the sky, he saw the thick grey clouds and then, the heavens opened.

Not wanting to risk entering the house until Kenny had given him the all clear, he darted to the shed at the bottom of the garden. He paused for a second, knowing that he risked his dad's wrath, as the shed was supposed to be off limits unless they were working in the garden. He decided it was worth the risk, rather than getting soaked.

Opening the door, he ducked under Charlotte's cobweb. He was fortunate enough not to be afraid of spiders, so he didn't mind the large garden spider that had made their shed her home. Well, it could be a girl. Zachary loved reading and had named the spider after the literary spider from E.B. White's famous book.

A glint of metal caught his eye as he moved inside. Zachary walked over and pulled back a heavy tarpaulin. His eyes widened at the sight. He picked up the axe and held it towards the window. There were stains on the metal blade, stains that were red.

"What the fuck are you doing in here, boy?"

Zachary dropped the axe in fright and turned to face the large figure of his dad, blocking the door. He felt his shirt being grabbed, and he was lifted off his feet.

"I told you not to come in here, boy, didn't I?" Zachary felt his dad's spittle drip onto his face. Harvey grabbed the boy by the middle of his shirt, holding him in his left hand. He raised his right and back handed the boy across his face.

Zachary bit back his sob, knowing that his dad hated crying. "I'm sorry Dad," he said. "It was raining, and I didn't want to get wet."

"That's not a good enough reason for coming in here."

Another slap followed by another.

Zachary had lost count by the time he passed into unconsciousness.

Chapter 16

May 2021

DI Michaels was having a déjà vu moment as the assembled crowd of volunteers combed the woods. The light from torches flashed in every direction as the names of Libby and Henry were called out.

He shivered as the memory of the search for Zack, some twenty years previously, sent a stark reminder about his first major case as a Detective Sergeant.

Ignoring the death of Mary Hopkins, the chopped up remains of Marc Wood had triggered his memory of the now infamous 'Woodsman' murders back in 2000 but, as Harvey Downes had been killed and the murders ended, surely the manner of the boy's death was just a coincidence.

"DI Michaels," Paula Smith shouted. "I've found them." Her voice sounded strained.

As he approached her, he could see a patch of vomit nearby. He gave her a look and saw that her face was a pale green.

"Are you okay, Paula?"

"No, no I'm not," she replied, her voice shaking. "We need to cordon this area immediately to stop anyone from the public getting in here and seeing this."

Will radioed through to the uniformed policemen and a perimeter was quickly established. He walked over to where Paula had indicated and pulled back the foliage. His heart sank. Body parts were strewn in a small area, almost as though the killer wanted the bodies found, which was so similar to the Woodsman modus operandi that it was eerie.

Darren Green arrived and quickly took charge, ushering out all and sundry as his team got to work.

"Are we sure its them?" Darren asked.

"Paula had the photos from Facebook," Will said. "It's them."

"Why have we suddenly had three schoolchild murders?" Darren asked. "I mean, I know Bristol had them murders twenty years ago."

"There's nothing to say this is related, Darren."

"But still ..."

"Still nothing. Get the evidence gathered up. I

expect a report on my desk in the morning."

Darren knew the tone of the DI brokered no arguing, so he turned and put his team to work.

North Avon Care Home was supposed to be the best in the area. The brightly lit corridors and airy rooms gave a comfortable feel, almost like a hotel. *Almost* Zack thought as he walked slowly towards his destination. He hated this place. Hated what it meant. Hated what had happened to his adopted dad.

Pausing for a moment outside the door to the private room, he knocked and waited for a reply.

"Come in."

Zack opened the door and felt his heart sink. Sitting in a chair, facing out into the sprawling gardens was Sammy Jacobs. The fifty six year old former teacher was a shadow of the strong man that had taken him under his wing some twenty years earlier. The only real father figure he had ever known, the only man that had ever shown him any real affection.

And now he was reduced to a shell of a man, sitting and gazing out at butterflies and clouds passing through the range of vision from the second story window.

"Hi Dad," Zack said, taking a seat to the side of him. He took Sammy's hand, and the man turned

169

his head. A look of confusion clouded his eyes.

"Ah, hello son," Sammy said, and Zack felt his heart lift. Did he recognise him this time? "Are you one of my students come for a lesson?"

"Not this time, Dad," Zack sighed. "I just wanted to come and see how you are, how you are getting on."

"Oh, that's nice. I do like it when I get a visit from my students. Now, what are we going to study today?"

Zack knew that it was hopeless trying to get his dad to remember him, but, as Uncle Will said, it wasn't just that, but that he should remember his dad and spend time with him, something that pained him every time, so he had stopped visiting.

Wanting to spend happy time with his dad, Zack spoke gently. "I think we said we would study 'The Wind in the Willows' today, dad."

Sammy's face lit up. "Oh, that is excellent. It is one of my favourite books, you know."

"I know, you said that we should study it this time."

"Well, let's start then."

"The Mole had been working very hard all the morning, spring-cleaning his little home."

The following morning, Zack walked into the

station and into bedlam.

"What's happening?" he asked Bobby as he handed his friend a plastic cup of sludge.

"Two more murders," Bobby sighed. "Libby Forrest and Henry Lavery were reported missing, and we've found them."

"What?"

"They were up on Brandon Hill. It's not good, Zack. They were chopped up just like Marc Wood."

"Shit. You don't think … ?"

A door slammed. DI Michaels walked into the office.

"Everyone. Conference room. Now!"

Zack and Bobby flashed a concerned glance at each other. Zack had not seen his uncle so upset and angry as this.

The team filed in silently, taking seats around the U shape table. Will turned on the screen and the gruesome photographs of the dismembered bodies of the two teenagers filled the screens.

"You could have warned us, boss," Bobby said, as he felt bile rising in his throat.

"This is what we are up against, people," Will hissed. "There is a maniac running around Bristol, killing kids, chopping them up. We have got to find whoever it is and end it. Now!"

"Boss, Bobby said that these are Libby Forrest and Henry Lavery?" Zack asked.

"That's correct."

"They were friends with Marc Wood. If I remember correctly, that lady, Mrs …" Zack paused as he flicked through a file. "Mrs Eileen Roberts who reported the attack on Oliver Williams put them both at the scene with Marc. If someone is taking revenge on Marc hurting Oliver, then it would make sense that they would go after these two as well."

"Not a bad call," Will said. "It gives us a starting point anyway. Look for connections between these three, Oliver and anyone else who would want to look out for him."

"Wait a sec," Bobby said. "These are Dan Hopkins' friends as well."

"What?" Will said.

"The kid from the Mary Hopkins case. Dan told us that he has a close bunch of friends that, in his own words, are bullies." He fished out a small notebook. "Marc Wood, Libby Forrest, her boyfriend Henry Lavery, which I guess is why the two were together on the Hill."

There was an enquiring look from the room. Bobby blushed.

"It's a known make out spot for teenagers," he explained.

"Oh, I remember catching you and Tracy Smith up there when we were fifteen," Zack laughed before seeing the thundercloud on Will Michaels' face. "Sorry. Bobby is right though. Dan's group also includes a Tony Gwynne and also his cousin, Philip Whitehall, would tag along with them, though he was more tolerated than anything else. I think that he gets the brunt end of their bullying."

"So, three out of a gang of six are dead, all of them known bullies," Paula said. "Doesn't this remind anyone of anything?"

The silence was deafening.

"Someone needs to say it," she said.

"We've got a copycat serial killer," Zack said. "Someone is copying the Woodsman."

"This is not spoken of outside of this room, do we understand?" Will said, a stern tone in his voice. "Once the press gets wind of that phrase, well, you only need to look up the archives to see the shit that we went through twenty years ago."

"So, are we looking at this as the working theory, boss?" Bobby asked.

"For the child murders, yes."

"Do we think this is connected to Mary Hopkins?" Paula asked.

"Find me a reasonable link, and I'll agree, but for now, that's still a separate investigation." Will nodded. "Okay, let's go and find this bastard."

"Come in Zack," Will said as Zack knocked on the office door. Will indicated to a chair.

Zack took the offered seat.

"Your gut is normally accurate, so what's it telling you?" Will asked.

"This is all connected somehow. The similarities are too much."

"I'll agree there are a lot of resemblances to 2000 but we know that Harvey Downes was the killer, and well, you stopped him."

Zack hung his head. "I still don't remember stabbing him."

"Don't blame yourself for that, Zack," Will said. "The way that we found you and your father, erm Harvey, it was obvious that he'd come after you and he tried to stab you. You must have somehow turned the knife on him. It was him or you."

"I just wish I could remember more, which is why I am here," Zack started.

Will looked at him, having foreseen this request coming.

"No, absolutely not."

"Withholding those files from me is hindering the investigations," Zack said, his tone hardening.

"It took your dad and me several years of therapy

for us to get you through what happened. I'm not going to risk a relapse."

"Uncle Will,"

"DI Michaels," Will said shortly, trying to establish the professional relationship rather than the familial.

"Boss," Zack said quietly. "You know I'm the best investigator on the team. I can see links and connections where others can't. I've proved that. Trust me, I won't let the past come back to haunt me. I'm over it. I know what my biological father did. But somehow, whoever this person is, he has inside knowledge. Dan mentioned a Charlie as to being the person that killed Mary, and that he was scared of him. I was looking back through my therapy diaries, and I make mention of a Charlie on a lot of occasions."

"It is just a coincidence."

"Then let me rule it out," Zack sighed in frustration. "It's playing on my mind, and I need to get rid of it so I can think straight."

"Fine," Will gave in. He wiggled his mouse to wake up his computer. He typed a quick email to the IT team to allow Zack's log on access to the files from the Woodsman murders.

Zack took a sip of lukewarm coffee as he read and reread the files concerning the murders of Jason,

Peter, George, and Ian. His mind flashed back to the bullying that he had endured at their hands. There were two files that he daren't open, not yet.

Picking up his phone, he dialled a number.

"Hello?" a male voice answered.

"Richard, it's me, Zack."

"Oh, hi Zack. Sorry … I thought you were another journalist."

"Damn, are you getting pestered?"

"Not as many now, but they are still calling."

"Look, I know this may be bad timing, but can I pop round? There are a few things I need to ask you."

"Is this about Mary? Dan?"

"Actually no," Zack paused. "It's about the past. About the others."

"Zack, are you sure?" Richard asked. "I don't think it's a great idea to revisit that."

"It could help with what's going on now," Zack said. "Please Tricky."

Richard laughed. "God, no one has called me that since …" he stopped.

"Since my dad died."

"Okay, fine."

Ten minutes later, Zack and Richard were sitting in Richard's lounge, looking at files that Zack really should not be sharing. Dan was upstairs in his bedroom, playing on the newly installed PS4 from the safe house with Philip and Tony.

"What I can't figure out is, why my father killed them?"

"Well, he was a bit nuts," Richard said. "And a drunk. Sorry."

"Don't be, it's true," Zack said. "He hated me, but why did he kill the others?"

"They were bullying you, so maybe he wanted to protect you?"

"But he hated me, blamed me for my mother's death, and like to slap and punch me," Zack argued. "Why would he have stopped anyone from doing the same?"

"I don't know. Maybe he had a sick way of thinking, you know," Richard paused. "Maybe he wanted to be the one to punish you and no one else could."

"I guess that makes some sense," Zack admitted. "But I don't buy it."

They sat in silence for a moment, sipping the whisky that Richard had poured them.

"Do you remember Charlie?" Zack asked suddenly.

"Charlie who?"

"I wrote about him a lot in my therapy diaries. But I can't remember him being part of the gang."

"We didn't have anyone called Charlie," Richard said. "Wait, there was Charlie Garfield, he was a bit of a nutter, but we never hung around with him."

"Charlie Garfield? Wasn't he that geek from Year 9?"

"He was a loner," Richard said. "But I don't think he knew you."

"Thanks Richard," Zack said, getting up. "You've given me a lead anyway. Dan mentioned a Charlie when Mary was killed. I think I'm going to find this guy and pay him a visit."

As they left the lounge, there was shouting from upstairs.

"Leave him alone!" Dan's voice was heated.

"You've never stuck up for him before," a voice unknown to Zack said.

There was a slam of a door, and the slim frame of Philip came running down the stairs. He had a large handprint on the left-hand side of his face and tears were streaming from his eyes.

"Can you take me home please, Uncle Richard," the boy sobbed.

"I can take him," Zack said, a protective instinct kicking in.

"Oh, hello Detective Jacobs," Philip said, wiping his eyes with his sleeve.

More shouts from upstairs and there was the crashing sound of a table.

"You go and sort out that mess," Zack told Richard. "I know where Philip lives. I'll get him home."

Richard nodded and headed up to the warzone as Zack led the crying boy to his car. Figuring he was tall enough for the front seat, Zack made sure that Philip was buckled in before pulling off the drive.

"Do you want to tell me what happened up there?"

"It was Tony being a jerk, again." Philip had stopped crying now that he was in the safety of an adult and away from the bully.

"What happened?"

"I beat him at Fifa and he didn't like it," the boy replied. "He wouldn't give up his controller to Dan, saying that I must have cheat codes. Dan told him to give his controller over and he threw it at me. Called me a fag and then slapped me."

"That's wrong of him," Zack said.

"I know, and so did Dan. Dan stopped him from hitting me again and Tony went mad. Dan has never stood up for me before."

"I think we are seeing a new Dan."

"I know, it's great. Dan used to be nice before he became friends with those others. Then he turned into a bully. It's like with Libby and Henry."

"What about them?"

"I was out walking and accidentally bumped into them. They were snogging and getting ready to have sex, I think. They saw me before I could turn away. They beat me up. Now they're dead as well."

"I'm sure it's a coincidence."

"I guess, but they were all bullies and now they are dead. I hope that Dan is okay 'cos he's nice to me now."

"I'm sure he'll be fine," Zack said as they pulled into the driveway of the Whitehall's house. "Now, go and clean yourself up before your mum sees you. She'll fuss all over you if she thinks you've been crying."

"Thanks, Detective." Philip flashed a bright, white toothed smile at him, ran to the door and let himself in.

Zack reached back and pulled his notepad back out.

"Charlie Garfield. Now, where are you at?"

Chapter 17

June 2000

Zachary woke up in bed. He had no idea how he had made it there. *Just another zone out I guess* he thought.

He stretched and immediately regretted it as pain shot through his body. Pulling back the bedcovers, he saw that he was dressed only in his boxer shorts. Purple and black bruises covered his chest and arms.

The shed! Zachary recalled his dad catching him in the shed and then the beating that followed. *I brought it on myself*.

Gingerly he swung his legs to the side and struggled to his feet. Wincing with each breath, he walked over to the bedroom door, opened it and looked up and down the landing.

The house was silent. Zachary glanced backwards

at the bedside clock and saw it was six thirty.

Dad will have left for work.

The bedroom door opposite opened and Kenny stepped out. He was sporting a black eye and was walking slowly. He stopped when he saw his younger brother.

"Zachary ..."

"You said you'd protect me." Zachary's voice was flat, unemotional, but the blame was there none the less.

"I tried. Dad beat me as well."

Kenny undid his pyjama top, and Zachary could see the green and black bruises forming around Kenny's ribs.

"We have to tell someone," Zachary's flat tone said.

"No, we can't," Kenny said, gasping slightly as he edged out of his room. "He'll kill us."

"Better dead than this," Zachary replied.

"No, it isn't," Kenny said. "When I'm eighteen, I can leave home and I'll take you with me, I promise."

"We'll be dead before then."

"Trust me Zack."

"Zachary is too forgiving."

"What? Why are you are saying it like that?"

"I don't care what you think," the flat tone continued. "I'm not going to let this carry on."

"We can't do anything." Kenny hobbled over to his brother. "Come on, let's get ready for school. I'll help you wash."

Kenny grimaced every time his brother pulled away from the damp cloth that he was using. Kenny was becoming increasingly worried about his brother's mental state. Even before, when Kenny had offered to help, the boy had always been independent when it came to cleaning up.

Today, Zachary had allowed Kenny to strip him and wash him. Kenny took his time, being as gentle as he could, but Zachary seemed to be in a zombie-like state, ignoring the attention his brother was giving him, except to pull away at a particularly sore spot.

He led Zachary back to his room and the boy stood there.

"Come on, you need to get dressed."

Zachary stared at him blankly.

Kenny shook his head and pulled out a pair of boxers and lifted Zachary's legs through the holes, pulling them up. He realised that he would have to fully dress his younger brother and did so, gently manhandling limbs through various openings before brushing his hair.

"I've gotta get myself ready," he said. "Why don't

you go downstairs and get some cereal?"

Zachary didn't answer but moved one foot ahead of the other. Kenny watched him walk robot-like to the top of the stairs. For a panicky moment, Kenny thought that Zachary might fall down but, instead, he placed a hand on the banister and walked down.

Kenny dashed back to the bathroom, washed himself as quickly as he could, even with the pain of the beating from the night before.

Walking into the kitchen, he saw Zachary eating a bowl of corn flakes with a bowl set out for him.

"Thanks."

"That's okay," Zachary said, his voice seemingly back to normal. "How did I get here?"

"You walked down dummy," Kenny tried to joke.

"No, I mean, I remember being in the shed, and Dad hitting me. I don't remember going to bed but I remember waking up. Then I saw you on the landing and then I was in front of the kitchen cupboards."

"You zoned out on me," Kenny said softly. "I washed you and dressed you."

Zachary blushed. "You mean you saw me?"

"Nothing we haven't both got," Kenny smiled.

"No, I mean the bruises."

"I know. I'm sorry. I promise I'll do better next

time."

"It's not your fault."

They ate in silence and left for school. Bobby went mad at the pair of them when he saw their bruises, but a stern look from Kenny was enough to silence the boy. As they approached the school gates, Zachary slowed his steps to a halt.

"What's wrong?" Kenny asked.

"Mr Jacobs is on the gate."

"So?"

"He asked me about the bruises last time and I told him I fell over."

"And that's what you'll tell him again," Kenny hissed. "If Dad finds out you've said anything, he'll beat you worse than ever."

"Maybe you should say something, and the police will make it stop?" Bobby butted in.

"You don't know my dad," Kenny hissed. "He's gotten away with this for years. He knows people. He's always been let off before."

They walked slowly to the gates. Kenny had positioned himself between Zachary and Mr Jacobs and all seemed to be going well. They said their farewells and headed to their respective form rooms.

Of course, this is where Kenny's plan was flawed. As soon as Sammy Jacobs walked into the classroom, he spotted the bruises covering Zachary's face, especially with the attention that Tracy Smith was giving him.

"I fell down the stairs, sir," Zachary lied. "I was running to get dinner last night and missed the top step."

Sammy knew he was lying but didn't want to cause a scene in front of the class. The bell rang to start the day, and Sammy was lucky enough to have Zachary for a double period as the first two lessons.

Zachary drew some attention from his classmates, several asking if the other kid looked as bad, the story of the fight with Freddie Kenton having done the rounds. He just smiled at them and kept his silence.

When the bell rang for the morning break, Sammy stood by the door and put a hand on Zachary's shoulder as he tried to leave. "Stay behind."

The boy's eyes met Sammy's and the teacher saw the pain. He resolved himself to help Zachary. When the class had cleared, he said, "come on, I'm taking you to the nurse."

"I'm fine sir," Zachary started but Sammy put his finger on the boy's lips.

"I don't think you are, so please, humour me. Let me get the nurse to have a look at you."

Zachary's will seemed to vanish as he felt concern and affection from his favourite teacher. He let the man lead him down three corridors until they reached the infirmary. Knocking on the door, he led the boy into the room.

Nurse Deacon was a maternal figure, beloved by the whole school. Her grey hair was pinned back, and she wore a hint of make-up. She looked like everyone's grandma with a disposition that matched. Despite the rules concerning sugar and sweets, she always had a ready supply to ease the pain of her kids, as she called them.

"Oh dear, what's happened here?" She immediately fussed over Zachary's face. "What have you been doing? Jumping out of trees and landing on your head?"

Her tone was such that it set the boy at ease, seeming to know that she wouldn't judge him.

"I fell down the stairs."

Sharron Deacon flashed a look at Sammy which showed her disbelief in the boy's lie.

"Okay sweetie, I want you to take your shirt off for me."

"Do I have to?"

The nod from the nurse gave the answer. Zachary gingerly loosened his tie, removed his blazer and hung it on the back of the chair. Then he undid the buttons on his shirt, pulled the tie over his head and took off his shirt.

Sammy's face hardened while Sharron's face paled as the extent of the bruising came into view.

"You must really have bounced off those steps, sweetie," she said, experience telling her to keep within the story that the child had given. "Let me get you some ointment for those bruises."

She stood and moved to a side cabinet. Finding a small jar of arnica ointment, she unscrewed the top and walked back over to the boy.

"This is going to be cold, I'm afraid," she said as she scooped a glob onto her fingers. Rubbing it gently onto the bruising, she took her time, noting where the boy flinched, making mental notes. Finally done, she told Zachary that he could put his shirt back on.

"I'd like to put another layer of the cream on you at afternoon break if you can come back, Zachary."

"Yes Nurse Deacon," the boy smiled at her.

"Okay, why don't you go and get some fresh air, but be careful, don't do anything that is too strenuous. You need to let those injuries heal."

Zachary nodded and left the infirmary.

"That boy has been beaten within an inch of his life," Sharron hissed at Sammy. "This has to be reported. We have a duty of care to our children."

"I know, I agree. I just couldn't figure out how to

approach it without Zachary panicking. Something is going on with that family and I am worried about what his father is capable of."

"Don't they have a second boy?"

Sammy nodded. "Kenny. He's in Year 9. You know those murders?"

Sharron nodded. "Terrible."

"All of the victims are friends of Kenny's."

"Is that a coincidence?"

"I don't believe in them."

"Can we get Kenny in? If he's being beaten as well, we have all the proof we need."

"Kenny's a tough nut. He won't volunteer to come in. I think he's the one telling Zachary to lie."

"Well, even without him, we can start the ball rolling. I will write up my report, and we do have the CCTV." She pointed to the camera in the right-hand corner of the room that the school board insisted on installing as part of their safeguarding concerns.

"My brother-in-law is a detective at Bristol Police. I'll give him a call and see what we can do."

The walk home that evening was one of silence and arguments.

"Why did you go to the nurse?" Kenny yelled at

Zachary once they had dropped off Bobby.

"Mr Jacobs made me."

"You should have refused."

"I couldn't. I told Nurse Deacon I'd fallen down the stairs like what you told me to."

"That's really bad English, bro!"

Zachary frowned and then stuck out his tongue. He put his hands in his blazer pockets as the wind started blowing stronger. "Oh shit, I forgot. She gave me this prescription. The school doctor signed it off."

"What? That means that they've got it on record now," Kenny moaned. "What is it anyway?"

"Some cream that she put on my bruises. It actually really helped."

"Dad's gonna flip. I'll see if I can get Tricky to get his dad to pick it up for us."

"I can forge Dad's signature. We can say he's in bed ill and I really need the cream. They should let us have it?"

As they turned the corner leading onto their street, the boys froze. Two police cars were parked outside their house.

"Shit," they said in unison.

"Jinx," Zachary said automatically.

"Don't be stupid. Come on. Let's see what's

happening."

They walked up the road and the boys recognised DS Michaels from the school assembly a few days previously.

A uniformed officer stopped them as they were about to walk up the driveway.

"Sorry boys, you can't come up."

"But this is our home," Kenny said. "What's happening? Where's our dad?"

Sounds of scuffling erupted as Harvey Downes was led handcuffed from the house. He spotted the boys. "What the fuck have you been saying?"

"Nothing Daddy," Zachary shook in fear as he saw the look of hatred and anger on his dad's face.

Will Michaels walked over to the two boys. "Maybe you should come inside for a moment." He led them into the home, and they headed straight to the kitchen. Zachary sat down heavily on a chair while Kenny opened the fridge door, grabbed two cans of cola and popped them. He poured one into a glass before putting two teaspoons of sugar into it and then handed it to Zachary. "Drink."

Will watched as the younger boy greedily slurped down the drink, wincing inside at the amount of sugar the boy was ingesting. He looked at Kenny.

"When he gets a panic attack, it helps to calm him down," Kenny said. "What's happening with our dad?"

"We had a report from the school about Zachary's injuries."

"I fell down the stairs."

"I'm afraid that the nurse and teachers don't believe that your bruises could have been caused by a fall," Will said gently. "It looks more like a beating."

"My dad doesn't hit me."

"Now, are you sure that's true?"

"Zack said it so, are you calling him a liar?" Kenny stood up, his chair scraping loudly on the floor.

"No, of course not," Will immediately recognised the stone wall he was going to encounter. "How did you get that black eye?" he asked Kenny.

"In a fight," Kenny replied. "You should see the other kid."

"Who is the other kid? Do we need to see if he is okay?"

Kenny felt the trap closing so decided to escape. "He's right in front of you."

"What? Zachary?"

Zachary looked up at his brother, realisation dawning on him that Kenny was plotting their escape route.

"Yeah, I broke his controller."

"I had told you not to come into my room,

squirt."

Will listened for a moment as the two boys traded insults and knew that, for now, he was beaten. Their father obviously had the pair frightened so badly that they would lie to the police to protect him.

"Okay guys, I'll leave it at that for now. Do you have anyone who can come over, or that you can go to, while we interview your dad?"

"I'm fourteen," Kenny said. "I'm old enough to be on my own and also to be responsible for Zachary."

Will nodded, not liking it, but knowing that Kenny was correct. "Fine, just make sure you eat properly and stay inside. Remember the curfew."

The interview with Harvey Downes did not go well. He flatly denied any wrongdoing, not even flinching when shown the camera footage of Zachary's injuries. He was pleased that his threats to his son had been heeded as he heard how Zachary had repeated time and time again that he had fallen down the stairs. His duty lawyer soon made mincemeat of Will's arguments to hold him, and he was released without caution.

Walking into the house, he found the two boys sitting at the kitchen table, plates laid out, including a place for him. The aroma of chilli con carne wafted through the house.

"We've made chilli, your favourite," Zachary said, standing up and walking towards the slow cooker.

"You did well today, boys," he said. "I believe that you didn't say anything to them nosey bastards."

"Of course, we wouldn't, Dad," Kenny said. "Family sticks together."

He felt touched for a moment at his first born's words before his eyes settled on the murderer. *Maybe the kid wasn't so bad. It's just that he reminds me of her so much, and of what I've lost.*

His heart hardened, refusing to allow the boy past the barriers enabling him to protect himself from that pain once again.

"Serve up and take yours upstairs," he said to Zachary. "Be thankful I'm not thrashing you again."

"But Dad ..." Kenny started only to be silenced by *the look.* Kenny sat back down and flashed an apologetic glance at his brother. He felt a growing resentment in his heart towards his dad. *He shouldn't treat Zack like this.*

Zachary served the two plates, placing them on the table and turned to head upstairs.

"Zack, wait," Kenny said. "You forgot your plate."

"I'm not hungry," Zachary replied in a sad, flat tone.

Zachary woke up hungry the following morning,

but at least his bruising was already fading with the ointment that Nurse Deacon had rubbed on him the day before. He made a mental note to remind Kenny to get Dicky's dad to get the prescription so he could continue to heal.

He got washed and dressed and met his brother at the kitchen table. Kenny had prepared a cooked breakfast, sausages, eggs, beans, hash brown and toast.

"What's this?" Zachary asked, surprised at the spread.

"You must be starving," Kenny said, as he dished up a plate. "Sit down and eat."

"I'm okay," Zachary started.

"Shut up and eat," Kenny interrupted. "Dad was wrong to make you go upstairs. I'm sorry, but I don't know what to do. I thought he might be okay after he knew that you didn't say anything."

"So did I," Zachary sighed. "But I guess he's never gonna accept me or love me."

"Well don't worry," Kenny said, squirming onto the seat alongside his brother. He put his arm around him and, with a slight hesitation, leaned over and kissed Zachary's cheek. "I'll love you enough for both of us."

Zachary's heart swelled and he fought back tears. For the first time in his twelve year life, he felt fully accepted by Kenny.

The walk to school was quiet, except for Bobbys' inane babble about the upcoming European Championship Final. Whilst the boys loved football, their interest in the Euros had ended along with the national team's dreams of success. Bobby loved football, any football and had watched every minute of every game. He chattered on about how Italy were so boring and that France had to be the favourites, especially with Zidane and Henry playing.

They arrived at school and the day started as the day always did.

Zachary ignored Mr Jacobs as he walked into the form room, deciding to join in with the football banter. Whilst Bobby was the font of all knowledge, Zachary followed enough of the Premier League that he could hold his own.

The bell rang for first period and Zachary got up to leave for his geography lesson. He saw Mr Jacobs at the door and tried to walk past him without making eye contact.

"Zachary, can you hold on for a moment please," Sammy said.

"No, I can't, sir. I can't believe you called the police on my dad," Zachary snapped at him.

Sammy was taken aback by the venom from his favourite student. "I was, we were just trying to protect you."

"You have no idea how to protect me. Only I can protect me."

Sammy watched the boy turn and walk away. He knew that there was something desperately wrong, but he was at a loss as to what it was, let alone how to help the boy through whatever traumatic experience he was encountering.

Zachary felt his head hit the locker, bringing him out of whatever daze he'd been in. He looked around. He was on the other side of the school from his form room. *How did I get here?* He started to wonder before a fist knocked the breath out of his stomach. He doubled over in pain, gasping for breath.

"You're a fucking freak, Zack!" Jack Cowell hissed at him. "Everyone who touches you is dead. You've got a demon inside you. Why don't you just do the world a favour and kill yourself before anyone else dies?"

"Maybe you shouldn't touch me then," a low voice came from Zachary's lips. "If you don't want to die as well."

Jack pulled away, staring at the boy in horror. Zachary's normally blue eyes had turned steely grey, and his face had hardened into a look of stone-cold hatred.

"You're a fucking freak, Downsey. Stay away from

197

me." Jack turned and fled, a chilling laugh following him down the corridor.

Chapter 18

May 2021

Zack sat at his desk and pulled up the logon page to the DVLA database. They were allowed to do basic searches without the need for a warrant, so he typed in the name 'Charles Garfield' but got a negative result. He knew that it wouldn't have been that easy. He tried various formulations of the name but with no luck.

"What are you doing?" Bobby asked, pulling his chair alongside Zack's.

"I went to see Richard last night and asked him what he remembered about the murders when we were kids."

"What? Why?"

"Something in my gut …"

"Your bloody gut!"

Zack ignored him. "Something is telling me that somehow these are all connected. I've been looking over and over at the reports for the murders and things just seem wrong." He paused and looked at his long time, best friend.

"Say it," Bobby said. "Whatever it is your holding back, thinking it's going to be weird or way out there."

"You know me too well. I don't think that my father, um, Harvey … I don't think he was the killer."

"What? Are you nuts? He tried to kill you, remember."

"I know, but he had always hated me. I don't get why he would have wanted to kill the others."

"Because he was mental and a drunk. My dad reckoned that he must have gone mad after your mother died."

"That's what everyone keeps saying, but some of the timings don't add up. Anyway, I went to see Richard and asked him if he remembered Charlie."

"Who's Charlie?"

"That's what I wanted to find out. Dan mentioned that Charlie killed Mary and that he was scared of him, and in my diaries, I mention Charlie a lot."

"It's a popular name."

"But that's it, it wasn't back when we were born.

It was only like, thirty fourth or thirty fifth."

"So?"

"So, Richard mentioned Charlie Garfield."

"Who … wait; wasn't he that weirdo who was the same age as your brother? He used to dye his hair black and wear nail varnish and make up and stuff. He gave me the creeps."

"Exactly. What if he was the killer?"

"So, what are you doing?"

"I was thinking that if I can link him to any of these deaths, then it could prove that my father didn't actually kill the others."

"What are you waiting for?"

"I can't find him on the DVLA database."

"He might not have a car?"

"How about National Insurance?"

"What are you doing guys?" DS Paula Smith interrupted.

"Er, nothing," they said in unison.

"God, you look like a couple of guilty schoolboys."

"I'm trying to track down a potential lead but can't find him. Bobby suggested doing a National Insurance check, but I'd need a warrant for that."

"Sod that," Paula said with the hint of a smile. She went to her desk and pulled out a tatty post-it note. "I'll need to rewrite this before it gets too crumpled." She handed it to Zack.

"What's this?"

"The boss's sign on. He has the authority to look without the need for a warrant in exceptional circumstances. He gave me his card when I was investigating the Burnham fraud case last year. His details accidentally managed to copy themselves onto this bit of paper."

"Strange how things like that happen," Bobby grinned.

"Come on, shift to one side."

Zack rolled his chair and gave Paula access to the computer. She pulled up the government records database and typed in Charlie's name. Adding filters, she quickly found the records that they were looking for.

"Well shit," Bobby said. "I guess that's that for Charlie."

Zack stared at the screen, not wanting to believe his eyes.

'Charles Howard Garfield. Born February 14th 1985. Died March 17th 2003.'

"Are we sure that this is the Charlie Garfield from school?"

Paula tapped a few more keys and the school records came up. It was the correct Charlie.

"Back to the drawing board, I'm afraid."

"Let's go get a coffee and some fresh air," Bobby suggested.

As the pair were about to walk through the doors, Will Michaels walked out of his office.

"What's up, boss?" Zack asked, noting the expression on his uncle's face.

"There's been another killing," he said with a hint of anger in his voice. "Darren is en route to the scene. I want you three there as well."

"Where?"

"The woods off Bellevue and Lower Clifton Road."

The three ducked under the yellow police tape that cordoned off the area, ignoring the gathering crowd of people who had stopped their morning commute to have a nose at what was going on.

"They are like vultures," Paula hissed. "Reality shows have made our lives a misery."

"It's human nature to want to wallow in the pain of others," Zack said. "There's more evil in the world than good. All we can do is try to keep it from overflowing."

"We're the good guys?" Bobby joked. "Tell that to the press. You should see the papers this morning."

They made their way along the path and spotted Darren Green. The chief of forensics was pulling off his gloves and had a pained expression on his face.

"I thought you'd be along," he said. "We've got another vic."

"Are you sure?" Zack asked. "It could be a different killer?"

"Nope. Same MO. The body has been chopped up with, I am guessing, a woodcutter's axe. I'll need to confirm the cuts back at the lab, but they look identical to the other vics. One weird thing though is that this was pushed into the boy's mouth."

He held up a clear plastic evidence bag. Zack grabbed it.

"That looks like a games controller," Bobby said.

"PS4 to be precise. Judging by the teeth marks on it, I would say it was in his mouth before the dismemberment started. The bite marks are quite deep."

"Can I see the head?" Zack asked.

"Why?"

"Have you ID'd him yet?"

"We haven't got that far. No ID on him, obviously as he's just a kid."

"I'm not a betting man but I would wager my month's salary that this is Tony Gwynne," Zack said.

"Why?"

"It's all repeating from before," Zack's face was pale as he spoke to them all and to no one in particular.

Darren led the trio past several trees and to the grisly scene. His team were carefully marking out the locations of the various body parts before gently placing them into the evidence bags to take back to the lab.

"Harry, where's the head?" Darren shouted.

"Over here, boss," a small man hunched over a tree trunk replied.

Zack walked over and took a single glance. "It's him."

"You know him?" Bobby asked.

"I know the group. It's all connected to the others."

"Let's get back to the station and tell the boss," Paula said.

An hour later, the team were all assembled in the conference room, a feeling of déjà vu spreading amongst them. The pictures scrolling through painted a macabre scene, one that matched the sombre mood of the room.

"Tony Gwynne; aged fourteen. Pupil of St James' school. Dismembered with an axe, most likely a short handled woodcutter. Body parts scattered in the same radius as the other victims. The only difference was that this boy had a PlayStation controller in his mouth."

"Why would someone do that?" Bobby asked.

"Because Tony and Philip Whitehall had a disagreement over who's turn was next," Zack said quietly.

"What? What do you mean, Zack?" Will asked, surprised at the depth of information.

"I was round at the Hopkins house last night talking with Richard. His son Dan, nephew Philip and Tony were in Dan's bedroom playing Fifa when they suddenly started arguing. There was a fight, and I took Philip home. He told me that Tony had kicked off because Philip had beaten him, and he was a sore loser. He slapped him around, but Dan stopped him."

"What has that got to do with this?" Will asked.

"Someone knew about it. They pushed a controller into the boy's mouth before killing him."

"Coincidence?" Paula asked.

"I don't believe in them," Will and Zack said in unison.

"Look at the others as well," Zack said. "Marc Wood was a known bully and had broken the fingers of Oliver Williams. He was found with his fingers broken before he was chopped up. Libby

Forrest and Henry Lavery. They had also beaten-up Philip because he caught them nearly naked, making out. They were found half naked, no sign of sexual assault by the killer but still, the similarity is there. Now we've got Tony, who had attacked Philip over a controller, and he is found with a controller shoved in his mouth."

"You can't think that Philip Whitehall is the murderer?" Paula asked incredulously. "He's what … eleven years old and about seventy pounds soaking wet. No way could he have the strength to overpower them and chop them up."

"No, it's not him. He's too sweet a boy," Zack said. "Besides, he had nothing to do with Oliver or Marc."

"So, what's your theory," Will asked.

"Someone is protecting the victims of bullying, and they have targeted Dan Hopkins' little gang of thugs."

There were murmurs around the room, some of agreement while others called it ridiculous.

"Okay everyone, settle down." Will turned to Zack and Bobby. "It may not be perfect, but it's the best idea we currently have, other than a random nutter running around. I want you two to go and have a chat with Dan Hopkins. See if he can shed any light. Paula, you take point on looking for any recent purchases of an axe and go back over the files looking for anything else that could connect these."

"What about Mary?" she asked.

"It could be connected, but doesn't fit the rest of the murders," Will replied. "So, for now we will keep that investigation separate. Paula, you still take the lead on that. I want Zack on lead on the kids."

"Yes boss," came the chorused response.

The drive over to the Hopkins house was quick and easy. Bobby and Zack mulled over the possible scenarios that Zack had suggested, in terms of who the killer could be.

"I hate to say it, but it's beginning to point towards Richard," Bobby said.

"It can't be. He was in the cells when Marc was killed."

"That could leave it at Dan's door. Now before you go off on one defending him, maybe what happened with Mary tipped him over. Seeing someone kill his abuser could have given him ideas about protecting other victims of abuse."

"I just can't see it," Zack said. "But I could be wrong. It's like I'm now convinced that my father didn't kill those kids back when we were young, but the evidence is there."

"Unfortunately, juries don't convict on the gut

feelings of the police. We need evidence."

They pulled up in the driveway of the Hopkins' house. The door opened and Dan came bounding down the path.

"Detective Jacobs," he smiled as he greeted Zack.

"Hey there, Dan. Is your dad home?"

"Yeah, we were just going to watch the game. Are you coming in?"

"Sure thing," Bobby said. "Who's on today?"

"Spurs against Wolves."

"Well, we don't want Spurs to win, do we?" Bobby joked.

They walked into the lounge and were greeted by Richard, who offered them a drink. With a cup of tea in hand, Zack got down to business.

"I've got some more bad news," he said. "Again, this isn't officially released yet, but will be by the morning. This morning we had a report of another body."

"It's Tony, isn't it?" Dan said more than asked. "That's the only reason you'd be here."

"It is," Bobby said. "I'm sorry, Dan. We know that he was your friend."

"There's something else," Zack said. "This detail won't be released, but he was found with a games controller in his mouth."

"What?" Richard gasped. "Why?"

"Last night, on the way home, Philip told me about the argument in your bedroom, Dan. How it started."

"It started 'cos Tony was a dick and called Philip a fag. He's not. Then Tony hit him, and I stopped him."

"I know you did, but that wasn't all."

"Dan?" Richard asked.

"I told you last night, Dad," Dan said. "Tony lost a game to Philip and wouldn't give up his controller." Realisation dawned in the boy's eyes. "You think that he told someone?"

"Maybe, or maybe someone else knew." Zack said, his tone suddenly less friendly.

"What are you saying?" the boy asked.

"Richard, what do you remember about the murders from before."

"What murders, Dad?" Dan asked.

"When I was your age, a group of boys were killed," Richard replied, his eyes hardening as he stared back at Zack. "I don't think it's appropriate to bring that up in front of Dan."

"Why not? There are a lot of similarities here."

"No. Your father is dead, Zack. He was the killer."

"I don't believe that and I'm going to prove it."

Bobby shifted uncomfortably in his chair. Dan's eyes had gone wide at the sudden confrontation between his father and the detective.

"Harvey was a psycho nutcase, and you know it."

"Just what was your role back in the day, Tricky?" Zack asked harshly. "You were the only one of Kenny's gang who was never attacked. That seems very strange, don't you think?"

"What are you getting at?"

"Everyone who died had bullied or attacked me in some way. Someone killed them for it."

"All I ever did was try to protect you," Richard snapped back. "And this is what I get?"

"You protected me by killing the rest of them," Zack stood up. "And you've now taken up the vigilante role again, haven't you?"

"Zack …" Bobby stood up, not sure how the situation had escalated.

"Richard Hopkins, I am arresting you for the murders of Marc Wood, Libby Forrest, Henry Lavery and Tony Gwynne. I am also advising you under caution that you will be investigated for the murders of Jason Billings, Peter Kenton, George Adams, Ian Hollis, Jack Cowell and Kenny Downes. You have the right to remain silent. If you choose to give up that right, anything you say may be used in evidence against you. Do you understand?"

"You can't be serious Zack?"

211

"Dad, what's happening?" Dan's voice trembled as Richard was grabbed by the former friendly detective and turned around. He watched as his dad was handcuffed.

"Zack?" Bobby started. "Are you sure about this?"

"Positive."

He led Richard outside.

"Sir, what's happening?" Dan asked Bobby.

Bobby saw tears welling up in the boy's eyes and he felt pity for the lad whom he had originally thought was a murderer.

"I'm sure we will get this all sorted out. Give your Uncle Jamie a call to come and get you while we sort this mess out, okay?"

"Okay," the boy said softly.

"Are you going to be okay until he gets here?"

"Yes sir."

"Zack, what the bloody hell have you done?" DI Michaels screamed at Zack as he slammed the office door behind him.

Bobby shifted uncomfortably in his chair.

"It all fits," Zack said. "Richard was the only one to survive the original Woodsman murders back when we were kids. He says he was protecting me, which is why the others died and he didn't."

"You know Harvey Downes was the killer," Will said in frustration. "We've been through this; this is why I didn't want you to have those files in the first place."

"Uncle Will, my father didn't do them. He couldn't have. He was too drunk most of the time."

"We don't have the evidence to hold Richard. He was in our fucking cell when Marc Wood was murdered."

"I hate to say it, but I think Dan is his accomplice. I think Dan murdered Mary, having finally had enough of being abused by her. Richard came home and found them. He covered it up and took the fall, knowing that he'd be cleared. Can't you see, it's the same pattern. All of the victims are bullies and Richard has a track record of standing up to them."

Will slumped down in his chair. He looked at Bobby.

"It does make a certain amount of sense, boss."

Will rubbed the bridge of his nose, trying desperately to fend off the impending headache that he could feel growing behind his forehead.

There was a knock at the door. Will waved Paula into the office.

"Boss, Richard Hopkins's lawyer is here and demanding his release. We either have to formally charge him or release."

"Uncle Will," Zack started.

"Zack, unless you have any evidence that we can prove, I have to release him on bail pending investigation."

Zack threw his hands in the air and stormed out of the office.

"Go after him, Bobby. You're his oldest friend. Get him to calm down," Will said.

"I'll try."

Two hours later, a calmer Zack was sitting in the brightly coloured room, staring out of the window at the flowered garden. Sammy Jacobs sipped at the glass of lemon barley water that Zack had poured for him.

"How are you doing, Dad?" Zack asked absently for the fourth time.

"Pardon? Oh, sorry son, I didn't see you there. Are you one of my students?"

"Yes, sir. Shall we read 'The Wind in the Willows'? I know that you like that?"

"Oh, that would be nice."

Zack started to recite the book that he knew by heart. He felt the tension and anger that had been building inside him start to melt away as a peacefulness came over him.

Why hadn't I done this more? All the time that I could have spent with my dad.

This isn't your dad. This is a substitute for the one we killed.

What? What are you talking about?

Harvey is your real dad and we killed him. We had to protect us. We couldn't let them know.

A hand on Zack's knee broke his thoughts and Zack looked at Sammy, a shudder running through his body as he tried to shake off that second voice in his mind.

"I recognise you," Sammy said.

"Thank God, Dad. It's me, Zack."

"No, no, you're not Zack. Your name is Charlie."

Chapter 19

4th July 2000

The bedroom door burst open. Zachary sat up, rubbing his eyes as Kenny charged in.

"What the hell did you say to Jack?"

"Huh?"

"Earlier at school. What did you say to him?"

"I don't know. He threatened me, said I should kill myself."

"I'll fucking kill him," Kenny snarled. "Why won't they just leave you alone?"

"I don't know. Jack said I'm cursed or something."

"Don't worry, bro," Kenny gave him a hug. "I've got your back, so has Tricky. If Jack comes near you again, you tell me, okay?"

"I will."

Kenny paused. "Why have you gone to bed in your clothes?"

"I guess I was too tired to get undressed," Zachary replied.

"Come on, get out and I'll help you undress. How are the bruises?"

"I don't really feel them anymore."

Kenny paused for a moment, his brother's voice having changed from the soft, gentle tone to a flatter, duller monotone. He shrugged it off.

"Come on, let's get you undressed."

Zachary slept fitfully that night. He dreamed of being chased by unknown shadows and started, sitting up, suddenly wide awake. He felt a dampness underneath him.

"Oh crap," he said but he was too tired, too exhausted and laid back down, falling asleep in the now urine-soaked bed.

His dreams continued, of the nameless shadows that seemed to be gaining on him, no matter how fast he ran. Just as he feared he was going to be caught, a new figure appeared by his side. Strengthened by this ally, he turned to face his foes, his fears vanished, and he slept soundlessly and peacefully for the rest of the night.

The following morning, as they reached the

school gates, the boys were surprised, but then again, not surprised to see the presence of policemen everywhere. They approached the gates and saw Mr Jacobs. Zachary headed over to him.

"Morning sir, what's going on?"

"Erm, how are you, Zachary?" Sammy asked, pleased that the boy was friendly towards him after their last conversation.

"What's happening, Mr Jacobs?" Bobby asked as the three boys jostled their way through the crowd of parents and students.

"The school is closed today, boys. You should head back home."

"Why?" Zachary asked.

"Who cares why," Bobby nudged him. "It's a free day!"

"What's happened, sir?" Zachary asked again. "There's been another murder, hasn't there."

Sammy paused. The teachers were under instruction not to tell the students unless they were with a parent. Sammy was well aware of the connections to Kenny and Zachary. He made a decision, and it would be a decision with which he would have to live with the consequences of for the next twenty one years.

"I'm not supposed to tell you but yes, I'm afraid so."

"It's Jack, isn't it?" Zachary sobbed. "Someone's killed Jack!"

Kenny looked startled at Zachary's outburst and sought a denial with a look at Sammy. The teacher's look only confirmed Zachary's statement.

"No!! I am cursed," Zachary shouted and collapsed onto the ground. He beat his head with his fists.

"Zachary, stop it."

"Zack, stop!"

Both Kenny and Sammy dropped to their knees to grab his flailing fists, but the boy was beyond reason. Desperation seeped into Zachary's brain and gave him an adrenaline rush that strengthened him beyond belief.

Punch after punch landed on his face and head as Zachary tried to beat the curse, the devil from him.

"Zack, please stop," Kenny cried. Tears flowed down his cheeks as he saw his younger brother unravelling in front of his eyes.

"Sammy. Is everything alright here?" Will Michaels asked, concern on his face. He recognised Zachary from the previous incident and his heart melted as he saw the breakdown in front of him.

Sammy had scooped Zachary into his arms, rocking him back and forth as if he was a small child. He stroked the boy's hair and Zachary seemed to calm down but was in an almost zombie-like trance.

"Sammy, take him home," Will said. "You're not needed here. There are enough of the faculty left." He turned to Kenny. "Is your father at work?"

"No. he's got today off."

"Okay, at least that means there is a parent there. Sammy, drop him off and come back once he's with his father."

Sammy picked up the now catatonic Zachary and headed towards the staff car park, with Kenny and Bobby in tow.

"Bobby, you get in the front passenger seat. Kenny, I want you to be in the back and hold Zachary. Keep talking to him. Let him know you're there."

"What's wrong with him?" Bobby asked, shocked at the reaction of his friend.

"I'm not sure, but I think everything has just overloaded him. I need to talk to your dad, Kenny."

Kenny just nodded, wondering what the reaction would be when they arrived home.

The reaction was not good. Harvey Downes' lip curled in disgust as he watched Sammy carry his son through the door.

"The boy has just been overwhelmed with everything, Mr Downes. I think bed rest should help him recover but if he is still like this at dinner time, I would call for an ambulance."

Kenny led Sammy through the house and upstairs to Zachary's bedroom. As soon as the door opened, the smell from Zachary's night-time accident was evident. He turned and opened the door to his own bedroom.

"Put him in my bed, sir," he said.

Harvey's face clouded as he looked inside Zachary's room and saw the large, yellow stain on the bed sheet.

Sammy laid Zachary down, stroked his hair once before turning back. He noticed the look on Harvey Downes' face, and he wanted to turn back, scoop up the boy and run as fast as he could.

"Mr Downes, listen. Your son has suffered a traumatic experience. You need to be gentle with him."

"I don't need advice on how to raise my son."

"You fucking do. I've seen the bruises. If you ever touch him again, I will kill you."

"You were the one who called the pigs on me," he said, realising who Sammy was. "Get out of my house before you're the one who will need saving."

Sammy was about to retort when Zachary moaned. They turned to see the boy stirring. He leaned into Sammy and hissed into his ear.

"I said get out of my house."

Sammy reluctantly left, seeing Bobby still in the car.

"Is Zack gonna be okay, Mr Jacobs?" The boy had tears in his eyes.

"I'm sure he will be. He just needs a rest."

Harvey Downes watched from Kenny's window as the teacher's car pulled away. He turned to see Kenny hovering over his brother.

"Go downstairs, boy."

"But Dad, Zack's not well."

"I said go downstairs. Do I have to take my belt off?"

Kenny's face paled. "No sir," he replied and slowly walked from his room.

"Shut the door."

The click of the latch sounded like the crashing of a tree that had been felled as Kenny slowly walked away from his bedroom.

He turned to look at the object of his anger, lying on the bed of his beloved son. His lip curled in disgust.

"Get up."

"I don't feel well, daddy," Zachary moaned in a soft voice.

"Get up and pull yourself together."

"I'm so tired. Let me sleep."

"Stop being a girl. Stop being a sissy. Get out of that bed."

"Please, just let me sleep."

"Get up and go to your own room. Go and lie in your own piss, you little shit."

He strode over to his son and grabbed the front of his shirt.

"You should have died instead of her," he shouted, spittle flying from his mouth, hitting the boy's freckled face. "It should be you that is in the ground."

"Well, I'm not," Zachary's harsh voice shot back. "No matter what you do to us, we will outlive you."

"Do not talk to me like that," he shouted, shocked that the boy actually had the gall to talk back to him. He released his grip and took a step back.

"Or what, Harvey? What are you going to do to us?"

"I'll …"

"You'll what? Beat us again? Belt us? Whip us? That's not worked before, and it won't work now. You are pathetic." The boy swung his legs over the edge of the bed. Standing up, he felt ten foot tall as he advanced on his father.

Harvey looked into his son's eyes and did not

recognise them. No, wait, just there. He had seen that expression before, those eyes. It was when the Billings boy had been killed and he whipped Zachary for answering him back, just like now. The boy had hit him around the head with that stupid trophy from his school.

"You little shit," he snarled as his hand dropped to his belt. Undoing the buckle, he said, "Drop them trousers and bend over the bed. You're going to get a whipping like you've never had before, Zack."

The boy sniggered. "Zachary isn't here right now, Harvey. You are done beating us. Zachary tried to get you to love us, but he is too weak, too forgiving. I told him time and time again it was a waste of time. You are a drunk; you have no love in your heart because you have no heart; you are a washed-up fool who cannot see what love you have in your life because you let hatred fill the void of the love that you lost."

"Don't talk to me like that."

"And worst of all, you're a bully. And Harvey … Charlie hates bullies."

The boy leapt forward and delivered a blow that was powered by twelve years of pent-up anger, twelve years of pain and agony, twelve years of longing for love and receiving only hatred.

Harvey fell to the floor and watched stunned as the boy turned and strode out of the room.

"Zack? What happened?" Kenny asked as he saw his brother stride through the kitchen. "Zack?"

The boy ignored Kenny as though he wasn't there. The boy wasn't interested in hurting Kenny, so he walked past him. The boy strode to the garden shed and opened the door. Brushing aside the cobweb that hung over the entrance, the boy strode to the back of the shed.

"What are you doing Zack?"

The boy pulled back the heavy tarpaulin, finding the axe that he so loved. He swung it, testing its weight, reuniting himself with the weapon. He turned.

"What are you doing with the axe, Zack?" Kenny asked, taking a step backwards.

"Zachary isn't here. You promised to protect him, but you didn't. So, I had to."

"Zack, you're not making any sense."

"My name isn't Zachary. I'm Charlie and I am Zachary's protector. Now move out of my way so I can do my job."

Kenny was rooted to the spot. He had a sudden revelation, and his stomach dropped, his heart lurched.

"Oh no, Zack," Kenny cried. "It is you, isn't it? You're the one killing the others. Why?"

"It's not Zachary, I told you. As for why? I told

you. Charlie hates bullies and you wouldn't stop them. So, Charlie did. And now, Charlie has to get rid of the last bully."

"I'm not going to let you kill Dad," Kenny said.

"Get out of my way, Kenny. Charlie remembers what you've done to us, but you turned a corner. You've been nice. Move out of the way."

"Or what, Zack, Charlie … whoever you are. Are you going to kill me too? You don't think I can take you. I've always been able to take you."

"That's when you were a bully and Zachary was a scared boy. Charlie is stronger than Zachary. Charlie hates bullies and Kenny, you have always been a bully."

The boy swung the axe upwards. Kenny saw sunlight flash off the silver edge of the blade and was transfixed. He watched the blade fall as if it was in slow motion.

A gut-wrenching scream came from the kitchen door as Harvey saw the scene in front of him unfold. The blade swung time and time again.

The axe was pulled from the boy's hands and Zachary gasped at the scene in front of him. His father was standing over his brother's dismembered body, a look of pure evil in his eyes. He turned and fled.

Branches scratched the face of the young boy as he ran through the thick copse of trees. All that he knew was that he had to run.

Chapter 20

3rd May 2021

Newly promoted Detective Constable Zack Jacobs drove down road after road. He was excited about tomorrow, which was to be the first day in his new role as a detective. Even more exciting was the prospect of working with his adopted uncle, Detective Inspector Will Michaels, who had been almost a second father figure to him.

He felt a twinge of guilt that he had been putting off the visit to Sammy, who was now at North Avon Care Home which specialised in dementia patients. He hated the time that he spent with Sammy, who had no idea who Zack was. It was as though another piece of his life had been hacked away, just like that of his brother when he was a child.

"Fuck Harvey!" he snarled as he gripped the steering wheel until his knuckles turned white. It had taken a couple of years of therapy to piece his mind back together after the attempt on his life by his father, who he had ended up killing in self-defence, but only after his father had murdered five boys as well as his beloved brother, Kenny.

He pulled up by the side of a road and wound his window down to get some fresh air to calm himself down.

Breathe Zack, breathe.

He started reciting lines from his favourite book, 'The Wind in the Willows', a trick that his therapist had taught him. Focus on something positive, something familiar.

"Leave me alone!" A boy's shout echoed through the window.

Zack looked around, trying to pin where the noise was coming from.

"You're fucking sick and I'm not doing it anymore." There was the sound of a slap on flesh and then a cry of pain.

Zack got out of the car and studied the street in front of him.

"No, I don't want to. Don't you dare tell Dad. Oh God, okay. I'll do it."

Zack's mind went blank as Charlie Downes took over. Charlie hated bullies, or anyone who hurt children. Charlie approached an open window and pulled a face at the scene inside. A boy of around fourteen, still in his school uniform was getting onto his knees. A woman who must obviously have been close to forty was hitching up her skirt.

Charlie went into the garden, took a pair of latex gloves from his pocket and put them on before trying the kitchen door. He eased it open just as he heard the woman start to moan. He crept into the kitchen and looked around. Picking up a heavy skillet from the counter, he tested the weight.

More moans came from the kitchen table.

"Leave the kid alone," Charlie threatened in a flat voice, and, as the woman turned, a look of shock and surprise on her face, Charlie swung the skillet. Over and over, he beat her until her screams died down.

"What's your name, boy?" Charlie said to the young lad who was trembling in fear underneath the table, his face hidden in his hands.

"Dan … Dan Hopkins."

"Well, Dan Hopkins, my name is Charlie and I hate people who hurt kids. You would never hurt a child, would you?"

Dan didn't answer.

"Would you?" Charlie asked forcefully.

"No, of course not," the boy stammered.

"That's good, because Charlie hates bullies and he would be angry."

Charlie left, taking the skillet with him.

30th May 2021

"I can't believe that they are going to get away with it," Paula fumed.

"You know, they could be innocent," Bobby said. "We have only got Zack's word that Richard and Dan did this."

"I trust him more than I do those pair. There is something not right."

Bobby bit his lip. He agreed that something wasn't right, but he wasn't sure that it was the Hopkins that were that something.

The door to the office opened and a smiling Zack walked in.

"Great news, the judge signed off on the search warrant." He held up the detailed forms in his hand.

"What's this?" Will asked, coming out of his side office into the open plan room.

"Justice Wesford agreed to my request for a warrant to search the Hopkins' home."

"When did you put that in?" Will asked, his voice hardening. "All warrant requests are supposed to come through me."

"I'm sorry, but I thought I remembered seeing

something out of place while I was driving home last night. You were out on a date with Auntie Tracey, and I didn't want to disturb you. I know what Auntie Tracey is like if you interrupt date night."

Will glared at Zack but said nothing.

"Okay, if you have the warrant and think you have proof, let's go get them."

They headed to their cars, with two pairs of uniforms in tow. Pulling up onto the driveway of the Hopkins' home, they walked up to the door.

Zack bashed heavily on the wooden door four times.

"Police. Open up. We have a warrant."

He turned to one of the uniformed officers who was carrying 'The Big Red Key' as it was affectionately known in the force. Sixteen kilos of solid steel, only the most reinforced doors could withhold its request for entry.

"Break it down," Zack said.

"Now hold on," Will started but the officer was an overeager thug who loved the power that he held. Will sighed as he saw the officer set himself and with a swing, the door splintered with a single, strong hit. He leaned back and followed up with two strong kicks and the door shattered.

They swarmed inside to the sounds of frightened shouts from the bedrooms upstairs. Richard

Hopkins, dressed in striped pyjamas rushed to the top of the stairs and gaped as he saw the uniformed officers rushing in.

Dan, clad only in boxers, trembled behind him

"What's going on?"

"Richard Hopkins," Zack said. "We have a search warrant for this premises in relation to the deaths of Marc Wood, Libby Forrest, Henry Lavery and Tony Gwynne."

"Not this again. You know we didn't do anything, Zack. My lawyer sorted it all out."

"Richard," Bobby started. "Zack seems to recall from the last time we were here some items that we need to have a look at. Let us just have a look around and, if there is nothing here, you've got nothing to worry about."

"I'm telling you now," Richard fumed as he came down the stairs. "You will find nothing here, and then I am going to sue you for continued harassment and whatever else my lawyer can think of."

"That sounds like a threat," Zack's voice went flat. "Sounds like a bully."

"Dad, what's happening?" Dan's voice was timid, scared. Zack almost felt sorry for him.

"Boss, we've got something." Paula's voice came from the kitchen.

They headed through to the kitchen where Paula was holding up a heavy metal skillet in her latex gloved hands.

"Where did you find that?" Richard gasped.

"At the back of the cupboard, hidden underneath the rest of the pans," she replied.

"That's been missing since, well, since Mary's death."

"Boss, there are blood stains on this. I bet we will find they are a match for Mary's."

"No, you can't think …"

"Bag it," Will said. His tone turned unfriendly. "I think you better start thinking about that lawyer, Mr Hopkins but not to sue us, but to start thinking about some type of deal."

A shout came from the back garden.

Will and Zack walked outside to see a uniformed officer holding up an axe.

"DI Michaels, I've got one of these at home to chop up wood for my firepit. It's a Topway 331212. There's blood on the blade. I've used it often enough myself. I bet it could easily go through skin and bone." The officer spat on the ground at Richard.

"That's not mine. I've never owned an axe."

"Shove it, Richard," Zack said. "As soon as we pull the prints from these and match the blood, both of you are going down for this."

"Dan hasn't done anything! You leave him alone."

"You've tried that one before," Paula snarled. "You'll soon find out how wife murderers and child killers are treated in prison. Your son is a little cutey, he's going to be very popular in prison. He'll have them lining up at his cell door."

"Get off me!" Dan's voice screamed as he was bent over the kitchen table.

Will stepped in. "Let him get dressed first; and then you can cuff him."

"Richard Hopkins, Daniel Hopkins. I am arresting you on the charge of murder …"

Richard's legs buckled beneath him as he heard the charges being read out. He screamed at the officer who was forcing a pair of shorts and a t-shirt onto the body of his crying son.

He looked at Zack, the boy who he had protected and saw a face he didn't recognise.

Charlie Downes smiled as he watched the police drag the protesting patsies away.

The brightly lit room smelled of lavender. Charlie Downes walked in solemnly followed by Doctor Hardy.

"I'm so sorry, Zack," the doctor said. "It seems that your dad passed in his sleep just after your last visit."

"It's probably for the best," Charlie said. "He hasn't been my dad for several years so, at least, now his soul is with God. Thank you for everything that you have done for him."

He shook the doctor's hand, ignoring the pillow on the bed that he had used to tie up the final loose end that could expose him.

Charlie held Auntie Tracey in a hug as the wake for Sammy Jacobs wound down. Tears had been shed, eulogies given, and songs sung in praise of a teacher who had touched so many lives, none more so than that of Detective Constable Zachary Jacobs.

"Well, Zack," Will said. "Have you given any more thought to your decision? Are you sure you want to go?"

"Yes, Uncle Will," Charlie said. "There are too many memories for me here. I'm just pleased that we have had Harvey's, my dad's, name cleared after all this time."

"I still can't believe that Richard had us fooled for all of these years," Bobby said.

"That's why he was called Tricky."

"Dan is being tried as an adult," Bobby said with a hint of regret. "He turns fifteen next week, so he'll be sent to Vinney Green. He better hope that he can defend himself or he'll be in for a rough three years."

"He shouldn't kill kids then, should he?"

"He's so young, and I actually started to like the little bastard."

"Richard was fifteen when he killed all of his mates, remember."

"I guess. I'm going to miss you, my friend," Bobby said, hugging the man he knew as Zachary Jacobs.

"I'll miss you too," Charlie Downes replied, and weirdly, with a pang of regret, found that he actually meant it. "You're one of the good guys, Bobby. Protect those who can't protect themselves."

"That's the job."

Epilogue

9th October 2021

Detective Constable Zachary Jacobs cruised around the streets of Nottingham, familiarising himself with the area. He knew it would take time, and while he had the benefits of the sat nav, he much preferred his own memories.

He pulled into the drive thru at McDonalds and ordered his favoured Big Mac, fries and a coffee. Pulling away, he found a quiet cul-de-sac and parked up.

Unwrapping his lunch, he munched away, listening to Classic FM and the sounds of the lunchtime show and the dulcet tones of Alexander Armstrong.

Peace and quiet. Life is good.

His musings were interrupted by the shouts of several young boys and the clattering of skateboard wheels on the pavement. *Kids eh?*

"Leave me alone!" a young boy's voice drew his attention.

He turned and watched as five boys, maybe fourteen had cornered a boy of no more than ten. The young blonde haired lad held his board tight to his chest.

"Give it up, Johnny, or we'll beat you."

The lead bully gave Johnny no chance as he lashed out a fist, sending the smaller boy tumbling to the ground. Laughing, he picked up the boy's skateboard and turned it over.

"Look at this beauty," he said. "It's wasted on a fag like him."

Charlie Downes fingered the newly unwrapped axe that had appeared on his lap.

"I've got your back, Johnny. Don't you worry about that."

THE END

ABOUT THE AUTHOR

Michael Andrews is a Birmingham based author and poet. When he is not tapping away at his laptop, you will find him watching his beloved Leicester City FC or sitting with his eyes glued to the latest Marvel production.

His books have sold to international markets, many gaining 5 star reviews.

He has been published in Cathartic Screams by Severance Publishing, had some of his anti-bullying poetry included in The Canon's Mouth and The Bullying Book as well as being a regular contributor to his local magazine.

Other Books by Michael Andrews

For The Lost Soul

The Empty Chair

Xeno

The Alex Hayden Chronicles

Book One: Under A Blood Moon

Book Two: The Howling Wind

Book Three: The Cauldron of Fire

Book Four: Dragonfire

Book Five: Children of the Sun

Being Alex Hayden

As part of JAMS Publishing

Words Don't Come Easy

Words Don't Come Two Easy

Words Don't Come Threely

Words Don't Come Forth

A Festival of Words

The Snarling Dog

Printed in Great Britain
by Amazon

85749923R00141